Fantasy. L   M

218 p. 1

undept dj: Ex lib.

scan?

$20.00

SO-BAK-548

686

5678734%

F
LEV

Levoy, Myron

Pictures of Adam

DATE DUE   14600

F
LEV   14600

Levoy, Myron
  Pictures of Adam

Pictures of Adam

Also by Myron Levoy

A Shadow Like a Leopard
Alan and Naomi
Three Friends

F
LEV

Pictures of Adam

by Myron Levoy

BLACKSBURG H. S. LIBRARY
PATRICK HENRY DRIVE
BLACKSBURG, VA. 24060

1   8   🖋   1   7

HARPER & ROW, PUBLISHERS

Cambridge, Philadelphia, San Francisco, London, Mexico City, São Paolo, Singapore, Sydney

NEW YORK

Pictures of Adam
Copyright © 1986 by Myron Levoy
All rights reserved. No part of this book may be used or reproduced in any manner whatsoever without written permission except in the case of brief quotations embodied in critical articles and reviews. Printed in the United States of America. For information address Harper & Row Junior Books, 10 East 53rd Street, New York, N.Y. 10022. Published simultaneously in Canada by Fitzhenry & Whiteside Limited, Toronto.
Designed by Joyce Hopkins
1 2 3 4 5 6 7 8 9 10
First Edition

Library of Congress Cataloging-in-Publication Data
Levoy, Myron.
   Pictures of Adam.

   "A Charlotte Zolotow book."
   Summary: Fourteen-year-old Lisa, a talented amateur
photographer, becomes involved in a bittersweet
relationship with an emotionally disturbed boy when
she does a photo essay on his run-down home up in the
hills.
   [1. Emotional problems—Fiction.   2. Photography—
Fiction]   I. Title.
PZ7.L5825Pi 1986   [Fic]   85-45268
ISBN 0-06-023828-3
ISBN 0-06-023829-1 (lib. bdg.)

14600

For Bobby and Lou

1

WHEN ADAM BATES was assigned the empty seat next to mine, three kids nearby called out *Oh, no!* loudly enough so that Adam, Mrs. Felts, and the whole science class could hear. And—I didn't want to believe it—Kim Wallach, my best friend, was one of them. I stared at her and she read my message. She turned red as a radish and looked away.

Nobody knew much about Adam except that he was weird and kept to himself. He was in a special class—"special students," they call these kids—and I guessed he was being released on good behavior or something,

1

like people in prison, to join our wonderful regular class in science. "Mainstreaming" is the nice ugly word they use. "Mainstreaming" and "special students." Talk about bull.

I've overheard teachers use those words. And words like "resource-room kids," which means about the same, and "learning disabled," and "emotionally disturbed." My cousin in Florida is all of those at once, and I think he's the greatest, so those fifty-dollar words, as my grandfather used to say, don't bother me much. People are people. Someday, when I grow up, maybe I'll do a study of kids like that. *Special Students* by Lisa Daniels. You see, in real life—which junior high school is not—I plan to be an investigative reporter, or I should say, a photojournalist.

Photojournalists don't just take news photos for the papers. They do a whole study of something, like drugs, or a war, or toxic dumping, or other nice things that adults do to set a good example for kids. I've been spending every penny I have on film and developer and fixer and enlarging paper. I develop my own film in my father's darkroom. He got me started as a shutterbug, as he calls it, when I was about ten. I think he's beginning to regret it. There were clearly negative vibes the day I spilled fixer solution all over the darkroom floor. And, lately, I spend so much time there that he can't do his own photos. It's been driving my mother bonkers, too. Not the money I spend, or the time, but the actual pictures I take. She thinks they're rank; I mean scuzz-bottom. So does Dad. He keeps talking about *painting* with a camera. About capturing the light just so, and the shadows, and the eternal beauty of nature, and blah blah. But I think old people sitting on a park bench can be beautiful. Or a battered car up on blocks. Or spiders.

I used to photograph spiders with a close-up lens. And spider eggs. And dead insects in the webs. And the spider working on the dead insect—dessert, I guess. I think *that's* beautiful: life and death happening right before your eyes.

But back to Adam Bates. Until that morning I'd only seen him in the hall once in a while, or in the cafeteria with other special students, talking to Mrs. Gladdings, the resource-room teacher. Sitting there next to me in science, he did seem a little strange. He kept staring at his desk with his science book opened to the wrong chapter. And his clothes, I must say, were extra grungy. I don't usually notice clothes; I dress like a slob myself, but the patches I've sewn on my jeans are neat and colorful. Adam's jeans were really in bad shape. One pocket was just hanging down, and he had a big rip right below his rear end. He didn't seem to care.

3

Adam was certainly different; what some kids call weird, and because he was, I wanted to try somehow to like him. Maybe because of my cousin, or maybe because I'm pretty weird myself. Everybody near him had hitched to the far edges of their seats, except me.

Adam kept looking at his desk while Mrs. Felts gave us the inside story on hemoglobin taking oxygen from here to there in our bodies. Then Adam noticed me staring at him, and I let him have my famous Lisa Daniels smile, which silences even barking dogs. He looked right down at his desk again.

The hemoglobin was getting complicated, and Kim, my friend, was looking at me looking at Adam Bates. I could feel her eyes from two rows over. She was obviously questioning my taste in boys. *Her* taste in boys runs to Russ Nielsen, which is perfectly okay if you like super-jock macho types who are strong, silent, and push you around. But, admittedly, exceedingly easy to look at in the sunlight.

Adam turned my way again, maybe to check out whether I was still staring at him, which I was. The Lisa Daniels smile reappeared. He seemed surprised, almost scared. His mouth dropped and he started to examine his desk again. Didn't people ever smile at him?

He couldn't be so shy because of my stunning beauty;

I'm what is known as ho-hum. Kim says I could be very attractive if I only did this to my hair and that to my eyes. I've tried it twice at Kim's house, and it took hours. My nose was still too noselike, my hair was still too bristly, my eyes were still too close together, and even with all that garbage on my face, I looked like the girl in the movies who always gets the laughs instead of the boy. I decided I'd rather spend the time on my photos.

Adam kept staring at his desk most of the hour. His mouth was still open; he seemed lost. Sad looking. He always looked all alone, even in the cafeteria with other special-ed kids around. Maybe that's why he was special ed; maybe he couldn't relate. Or maybe he was very unbright. Or really had some loose screws. Or all of the above.

I have a bad habit of looking at people from the viewpoint of how they would photograph. Adam was thin and wiry, not really muscular like Russ Nielsen who, Kim tells me, lifts weights. And Adam wasn't all that tall either. But his face was very interesting, in a sandy-haired, snub-nosed sort of way. Very expressive. I would love to capture the shyness there, that lost look.

He turned toward me a third time, looking a little guilty, as if he were embarrassed to be noticing me noticing him noticing me. Figure that one out. I smiled again, leaned toward him across the aisle, and whispered, "Hi. I'm Lisa Daniels. Hi. Uh . . . I think you're in the wrong part of the book. We're on page two twenty-seven. You know, the hemoglobin baloney?"

His eyes went down toward his hands. "I d-don't care," he whispered. "We don't have hemoglobin. But th-thanks." He had a slight stutter.

"Huh?" I said. Maybe he meant they don't teach about hemoglobin in special ed. "Well, we're studying it here," I whispered.

He shrugged. Then he looked at me squarely, as if he was trying to figure out whether I was okay and he could trust me. His eyes were gray-blue and busily bright. Not dull at all.

Finally he whispered, "You don't understand. It's not important for m-me, because we don't have any hemoglobin where I come from."

Pretty strange. He shrugged again, and I shrugged back. How could anyone live without hemoglobin? Very intriguing.

"Didn't you have to breath oxygen when you were little?" I whispered. Was Mrs. Felts looking our way? No, thank goodness. She'd started drawing part of the hemoglobin molecule on the board. But some of the

6

kids were looking at us, including Kim.

"N-no," he whispered back. "Because all we had was water. We lived in the water."

"But there's oxygen in water," I said.

"Not where I come from. It's a different c-chemistry. I've been reading up on it at the library." He had to be putting me on. Maybe this was his way of teasing. His eyes almost gave him away.

I decided to act as if he were serious. "Oh, really? The library? Are there books on it?"

"It's not in a book yet," he whispered too loudly. "Everybody's just discovering it now—the place I came from. But it's in the science m-magazines. I go to the library all the time. To check how close they're getting . . ."

"Are you going there today?" I'd never noticed him at the library. Then again, I'd never looked.

"Sure . . ." he whispered. His eyes were down, studying his hands some more. "Uh, don't tell anybody else what I said. Nobody knows about it. They'll l-laugh at me." Again, he stared right at me, searching for me to say the right thing. His mouth had a little twist of hurt now, like a kid who's been unfairly punished.

"Don't worry. I won't breath a—"

"Lisa and Adam!" Mrs. Felts called from the side

7

blackboard, her chalk in mid-molecule. "Would you mind! I'm trying to teach! You should know better, Lisa! Both of you! Please!"

"I didn't do an-an-anything!" said Adam, looking very scared.

"I—well . . ." said Mrs. Felts, clearly thrown by Adam's reaction. "Just please don't whisper in the middle of—"

"I didn't do an-anything! I didn't! I *didn't*!" He sat rigid in his seat. Everybody turned toward him; you could hear the proverbial pin drop. Talk about tense.

I felt as if I'd broken a window and Adam was taking the rap for me. It was all my fault, all those stupid questions. You don't fool around with people who have problems.

Mrs. Felts looked slightly ill. "I'm not going to punish you—"

"I didn't! I didn't do an-anything!"

I leaned over to Adam and put my hand on his wrist. "*Ssh*. It's okay," I whispered. I think the whole class could hear me; it was that quiet in the room. "It was all my fault. It's okay. It's okay. . . ."

He relaxed a little, and as he eased back in his seat, Mrs. Felts actually nodded toward me and gave me a grateful smile, breaking her latest nonsmiling record of eleven days, six hours, and twenty-seven minutes.

8

Adam just stared at his desk again. Any normal person, like Kim, would at this point have decided that Adam Bates wasn't exactly the best bet for a developing friendship. I guess even I had to admit it. But, in spite of everything, there was something about him. Maybe he was strange, but he seemed to be—how can I say it—his own self. What I mean is that Kim's super-stud boyfriend, Russ, is always imitating someone else: Matt Dillon, or Prince, or Tarzan of the Apes. It's like he's saying look at me! I'm tough, cool, and sensational. So many of the guys seem that way. They all put on this act. I guess I sort of liked Adam for not being like that. For his shyness and even that hurt look he'd suddenly gotten. Or did I just feel sorry for him? Where does one feeling begin and the other end? I couldn't really tell.

2

I TALKED KIM into biking with me to the library after school. First of all, I'd heard there was an announcement for a photo contest on the board there. And, second of all, there was Adam.

Even on a bike Kim manages to look great. When I'm on a bike I look dedicated to biking. Whatever I do, wherever I go, I always look intense and dedicated. Maybe it's because I really concentrate on what I'm doing—mouth tight, eyebrows knit—or maybe it's because I don't have the right curvatures. But Kim's amazing; she seems to ride a bike like a belly dancer,

10

and boys turn to stare at her. Life is not fair.

But I don't really care; my eyes are over the next mountain, as Grandpa used to say. My grandfather died last year. Oh, brother, do I miss him. When we used to talk, he didn't seem any older than me. Strange. My dad's father sometimes actually seemed younger than Dad. Anyway, I look ahead. I plan to be the next Dorothea Lange someday—she was a very famous photojournalist—while Kim plans to be . . . what? She doesn't plan. Sometimes she says actress, sometimes interior decorator. It depends on her mood. She's so laid back. I envy her; I'm always biting my fingernails, waiting for the next disaster.

As we biked single file along Lake Hills Avenue, Kim called out to me, "You know he's crazy, Lee!" Meaning, of course, Adam. Yes, it had slipped out that I knew he'd be at the library.

"I don't care!" I called back.

"You'll be sorry!"

"I'm not marrying him, you know!"

"You'll find out!"

We kid around like this a lot while we bike, only I think Kim was serious this time.

"I'm curious about him, that's all!" I shouted back to her. "I think he's . . . interesting!"

"He's not all there!"

11

"None of us are! Present company included!"

"You like him because he's got sexy eyes or something. Tell the truth!"

"When you tell me about Russ!"

"There's nothing to tell!"

"That's not what I hear!"

She pulled her bike up alongside of mine. "What? What did you hear? Who's talking about us? Lee, tell me!" This wasn't the usual Kim Wallach that I know and cherish. She normally never gets flustered. My little joke had gone too far, I guess.

"No one's talking about you. I was kidding."

"Lisa!"

"No one!"

"You swear?"

"Yes!" Oh, wow. What was she so worried about?

The library is always farther than I think. By the time we got there we were both wiped out from biking. The poster about the photo contest was on the big bulletin board just past the main door, and it was great! It was for a contest sponsored jointly by the Lake Hills Township Library and the Lake Hills *Daily Sentinel*, our local rag. There were to be four categories: single black-and-white photo; single color photo; portrait, color or black and white; and photo essay. Yowie! That last one was for me! No professionals permitted; no one connected with the library or newspaper; submissions

12

by May 31; name, address, phone number on back of each print. Awards: first prize in each category, two hundred unbelievable dollars; second prize, fifty dollars; third prize, twenty-five; ten runner-up prizes, two rolls of film. All *right*!

There was a pad of entry blanks on the long table near the door. I was so nervous, I tore a blank in half as I pulled it from the pad. Kim pulled two applications off and handed them to me.

"Hey, are you joining, Kim?" I asked. I forgot to mention; Kim's been doing some photography, too. Influenced by me, I guess. Only she tends to photograph kittens and flowers. My mother loves her stuff. But Kim's okay; I'm educating her slowly. I'll have her taking pictures of raw sewage within a year.

"Not me," she said. "I just figured maybe you could enter twice like in a lottery."

"Kim!"

We started browsing among the book aisles. If Adam Bates was somewhere in the library, I wanted him to see me looking at books so he wouldn't think I was there just to hunt him down. Besides, I like browsing in bookstores and the library. I like it best in New York City because the bookstores there have huge sections on photography. I stand around thumbing through the oversized photo books until Mom drags me bodily away. Eisenstaedt, Cartier-Bresson, Walker Evans, Margaret

13

Bourke-White, Dorothea Lange—I like them all, though Lange is my all-time favorite. I'll tell you more about her later maybe.

So we were browsing. Kim was surveying the human sexuality section, trying to see what kinky things they'd missed in the sex-ed course at school. Every so often she'd urgently call me over for another great revelation. Such as some people can only make love in dangerous places like in lion's cages, or on the wings of an old-time airplane, or whatever. I said that it must lead to very short romances, but Kim didn't appreciate my little insight. While I stood there a woman came down the aisle, and Kim grabbed a book from the opposite shelf and started reading about the history of the union movement in the South.

Poor Kim, I worry about her. I may not be able to do a belly dance on a bike, but I'm not hung up about sex, either. It's there, and someday I intend to enjoy it when I'm ready for it—the real *it*, of course. When Kim asks, I usually say college is my crossover point. No danger, anyway. I'm still working on my first kiss from someone other than aunts and parents. Sweet fourteen and never been kissed. Well, maybe not sweet. But never been kissed. I'd settle for just rubbing noses with someone. Through a plate-glass window.

But if everything is going so peach ice cream for

Kim, why had she been so upset before, when we were biking? And why does she pore through all those books? Maybe she—multiple choice: a) is worried that he/she wants to do more; b) is doing more, but isn't telling me about it because it's none of my business; c) is thinking of renting a lion's cage.

So there we were, browsing, when I noticed Adam sitting off in a far corner of the reading area. Had he seen me? Probably not; he was too busy staring at a huge book. I grabbed a book myself on the life of Alfred Stieglitz, another big-name pioneer photographer, and nonchalantly walked to Adam's table and sat in the chair opposite his. Very casual and cool, right?

Adam still didn't seem to notice me; he was totally absorbed in his book. I strained in my chair to see the book better; it looked like some kind of an astronomy textbook with star photos and graphs and tables. One thing was clear: either Adam was using the book as a doorstop for his brain while sleeping with his eyes open, or else he was a lot smarter than anybody thought.

He saw me at last and that shy look came over him again, like a blushless blush. I could feel it go through me like a wave.

"Hey, hi!" I said, with my glorious gift of gab.

"Uh . . . uh . . . hi. . . ."

15

"I couldn't help noticing your book," I said, half sprawled across the table.

"It's—it's . . . I have to learn everything in it," he said.

"Oh. For school?"

"No. For me. This tells how to locate any s-star you want any time of the year. And it has photographs of them. Want to see?"

"Sure."

He turned some pages, and I could see by the way he flipped back and forth that he knew this book inside out. He stopped at a page with a photo of two or three dozen stars, some very bright, and some just tiny sparks. He pointed to the brightest of them all.

"See? Right there. That one. It's Vega, or actually it's called alpha Lyrae. It's an AO-type star and it's 26.5 light-years away. It's got an intrinsic b-brightness of 0.5, which means it's very b-bright."

Obviously that star wasn't the only thing that was very bright. Why was Adam in special ed? I guess it had to be for things like that outburst in the classroom and staring at his desk all the time instead of reading the textbook.

"That's interesting," I said. "You're really into astronomy, huh?"

"Yeah. I read about it a lot."

16

"Uh . . . Hey, let me ask you something. In class today—you were kidding about that oxygen stuff, right?"

"N-no. That's what it's like where I come from."

"Oh, okay. Then where's the magazine you said it was in?"

"I c-can't tell you any more. I shouldn't have told you anything at all."

He was looking down at the astronomy book, and did he seem nervous! I felt guilty, as if I'd entrapped a little kid into facing a lie.

"That's okay," I said. "I know you're just kidding. . . . I guess I'm slow. I don't always get it when somebody's pulling my leg."

He looked straight at me, as he'd done in class. "But I wasn't kidding."

"Oh, come on. Nobody can live without oxygen. Where can you live without oxygen?"

There was this long pause, while he seemed to be thinking something through. He looked down at the astronomy book, then back at me.

"The only p-people who know where I come from are my mother and sister. Okay? Because they wouldn't make fun of me. . . ." He paused again and stared right at me as if begging something. He had that same hurt twist to his mouth I'd caught in science class.

"Do you think *I'd* make fun of you?" I asked.

He was looking right into my brain, I felt. That moment seemed to last for minutes. Then he shook his head no. He pushed the astronomy book across the table to me and pointed at the black space around that star, Vega. "I come from th-there."

"What!" Oh, wow. There was your special-ed story, I thought.

"There's a planet there," he said. "It's my planet, Vega-X. I call it Vega-X because I don't know its real name. It goes around Vega once every eighteen years. I f-figured it out."

Maybe he was still pulling my leg; he seemed to be making it up as he went. But no. That look in his eyes. No, he believed it.

"It's just all black," I said, trying to be gentle with him. "I can't see a thing there."

"That's just a regular star photo. You've got to have infrared d-detectors to see it. Look at this."

He took an envelope out of his pocket; the envelope was crammed with clippings from newspapers and magazines. He plucked a worn clipping out and pushed it across the table to me. It was from the Lake Hills *Daily Sentinel*. The article described how there was a planetary system developing around—you guessed it—Vega. It said they could tell from measurements using something called the Infrared Astronomical Satellite. You couldn't see anything with normal telescopes, but they could calculate what was happening from infrared heat measurements. Still, it only said planets *developing*.

Adam seemed to sense my question, maybe because my brow was knit more than usual. "They're wrong about some of it," he volunteered. "But they're g-getting closer and closer to the truth."

"What truth?" I asked. Now *I* was the nervous one. He couldn't have prepared all those clippings just for me; some of them were worn with use. He really, really believed this stuff. I didn't want him to be crazy. It's just a vivid imagination, I thought. What an imagination. . . But Kim would have called it crazy. So would Mom. So would Dad.

"What truth?" I asked again.

"That there's another civilization out there. If they weren't so stupid, they'd be reading m-messages from Vega-X by now. But they don't know how."

"Okay, if you're from this planet Vega-X, how did you get here?" Could he come up with an answer that made sense? I half-wished he actually *was* from another planet and could prove it. I guess I still liked him and I was trying to make it all normal somehow . . . like my aunt and uncle keep trying with my cousin.

He pushed another clipping toward me. It was from *The New York Times*, about how the basic chemicals of life, the stuff in DNA and RNA—cytosine, adenine,

19

thymine, guanine, and uracil—had been found in a meteorite.

"See?" he said. "There's stuff coming from outer space all the time. From my planet and other planets, all the time. They send it in m-meteorites. And in cosmic dust. And once in a while they send stuff in space c-capsules, too. For a soft landing. And sometimes even living beings, like me."

"Wait! How do you suddenly go from meteorites to space capsules?" At least he was trying to explain things. Crazy people don't try to explain anything, do they? I hoped not.

"How do you get thy-thymine and adenine and all that inside a meteorite?"

"I don't know. But I've seen meteorites in the Hayden Planetarium in New York. I've never seen a capsule from outer space."

"I can show you a space c-capsule. It's the one I was in when I was a little kid. It's up on the hill near my house. I dug it out last year."

Nuttier and nuttier. "Okay. Show me!" Put up or shut up, I thought.

"We can go there after school tomorrow."

"How about now?" I asked. Kim had just come over and was standing there trying to get the drift of our talk. Thank goodness she hadn't heard the whole conversation.

20

"Uh—we can't go now. I've got to f-fix things up at my house," said Adam.

"Okay, tomorrow," I said. "I'll meet you in front of the school's main entrance at two-thirty sharpola. Okay?"

"Okay."

What was I getting into? Going to look at his space capsule? Nutso squared. I sometimes am a bear of very little brain.

Kim hovered near our table. "By the way," I said to Adam, "this is my friend, Kim Wallach. Kim, this is Adam Bates."

"Hi," said Kim, cheery as a quiz-show hostess.

"H-hi."

"And, in case either of you have forgotten, I'm Lisa Daniels. Hi!" I waved both hands like a cheerleader.

"Hi," he said, looking suddenly shy again, probably because of Kim. Or because of my crazy exuberance.

"Okay," I said. "I'll meet you two-thirty, *mañana*."

Which left Kim out, I know. But Kim understands. She *over*understands. As we left the library, she said, "His house? I hear he lives way up in the woods somewhere. Nobody would hear if you screamed."

Beautiful. That was all I needed. She was probably right, and I was obviously nuts to go, but I resented her saying that, anyway.

21

"I'll take a whistle with me," I said, in my best sarcastic voice. But then she said something that really bothered me.

"Well, don't expect me and Russ to go out with you guys, or anything."

"I'm not going out with him!"

"Oh, come on, Lee!"

"Why wouldn't you go out with us? Because he's in special ed? He happens to be very bright. He can match Russ any day. And he doesn't have to wear a black leather jacket and sunglasses all the time to feel good, either."

"Thanks a lot, Lisa! Leave Russ out of this, okay?"

"Okay. Okay."

"Lee, listen to me! That guy, Adam, is weird. He's just weird. Look how he was in class. Lee, stay away from him!"

"No, I won't," I said glumly. I could see Kim's point in warning me to be careful about going to his house. I was worried myself. But I couldn't see the going-out bit. Kim was supposed to be my friend, and if, *if* I ended up accepting Adam—as a friend say, just a friend—and Kim boycotted him, it would mean she didn't accept *me*. Or my judgment that he was okay. Or my taste. What kind of friend is that, I wondered, as I gloomily rode my bike home.

22

3

THE WALLS OF my room are covered with photos. I've put my best ones up, including an enlargement of my famous spider. I've put up a few of my father's pictures, too, all misty and soothing, the sort you see in posters with inspirational messages like "every day is a new beginning." And I even have one of Kim's photos above my desk: daffodils, just blooming. That afternoon I felt like taking her picture down and sticking voodoo pins in it.

When I get angry or depressed I lose all my energy. I just lie there on my bed, sulking. I may be imitating

Mom; she does the same thing. The problem is, when Mom's feeling down, she mixes herself a big vodka martini, which makes her even more depressed. I'd noticed when I'd gotten home from the library that she'd already had one. I can usually tell; she seems to move in slow motion.

As I stretched out on the bed I glanced at the photos on the wall, then at my desk covered with cameras and junk, then at the floor covered with clothing and more junk. I understood why Mom gets so upset every time she comes within ten feet of my room. It is a total, unspeakable mess. Kim sometimes asks me to blindfold her before she comes in, so she doesn't have to see it. Mom's given up; she doesn't come in at all, if she can help it.

We have this problem, Mom and I. She is neurotically neat, while I'm sickeningly slobbish. Our living room is full of glass cabinets and beige carpets and Mom's collections of delicate seashells and antique paperweights, everything arranged beautifully with pinpoint lighting effects. Even our main bathroom has a perfectly symmetrical display of seashells and paperweights on shelves next to the mirrored cabinet. Mom's more than neat; she's fastidious. Sometimes I think she's nuts.

Dad's more like me, when he's not on his Madison

Avenue job in New York. The only place at home where he's neat is in the darkroom, where I, sob, am still a slob. Yes, that rhymes.

Anyway, looking around my room made me feel worse, so I vowed to clean it up. Soon. But not too soon.

There I was then, feeling sorry for myself, without the get-up-and-go to fill out my photo contest entry form, when Mom called to me from downstairs. "Lisa, you're supposed to help me with dinner tonight!"

Oh, sugar. She was right! I help make dinner Tuesdays so Mom can get dressed and get out to her modern dance group, and also so I can learn how to cook. Yes, friends, my mother insists that I master the art of Chicken Kiev and Fettuccine Alfredo, not to mention Hamburger New Jersey. I've made speeches to her about the women's movement, and old-fashioned stereotypes, and my allergy to cooking anything more elaborate than a peanut-butter sandwich, but it's hopeless. Mom used to be a home-economics teacher before she got married and won me in the jackpot. And she believes that cooking, sewing, and neatness constitute the three-fold path to survival.

Her second call was louder and sharper. "Lisa! How about it!"

I raised myself slightly for the return shout, "Okay!

25

I'm coming!'' Then I slumped back on the bed. I tend to be a three-call type, though it's living on the edge of danger. Kim is a one-call weakling, but then again, her mother always speaks calmly and softly, which is a lot scarier than my mother's shouts. I have a feeling that if Kim didn't jump, her parents might just tear up her birth certificate and renounce her as unfit to bear the family name. Her parents have her kid brother, Danny, jumping, too. There's something wrong somewhere. Probably with me.

The third call was close to pleading. ''I need you down here! Lisa! Please!''

I was out of the bed and on my way. I could hear the dry martini in her voice now. I suddenly felt sorry for her; she had such a pain for a daughter. And she and Dad were having arguments; about what, I don't know. I can hear their blurred voices sometimes when I'm falling asleep; they seem to wait till I'm in bed. Three or four kids I know have divorced parents, and I wonder if it's happening to me without my knowing it, like those houses you see on the TV news that sink overnight into an underground cavern.

Our kitchen is huge and over-equipped with every latest gadget known to humankind. Par for an ex-home-ec teacher, I guess. Mom was in the middle of preparing shrimp Cantonese style; there were peeled and

26

unpeeled shrimp in two bowls, beaten egg in another, cornstarch in a cup, and scallions in a little dish. Totally organized. She sat at the counter studying the book of Chinese recipes. Her martini glass was next to the peeled shrimp. Her eyes looked red and slightly swollen.

"It's about time, Lisa, don't you think?" she said quickly, like a teacher trying to control her classroom. "All right. Please read the recipe, then finish peeling the shrimp. And they all have to be deveined. And after that—"

"But they don't usually devein them in Chinese restaurants," I protested. Mom uses the word "devein" for the removal of the thin black intestine, or whatever it is, along the back.

"That's why we never order Cantonese shrimp when we eat out," she said.

"But it's perfectly safe!"

"Lisa, I'm not in the mood to argue with you. There's more than safety involved. It's safe to eat fried grasshoppers. But it's aesthetically repugnant to me, if not to you. Okay?"

"Okay." Her voice sounded fine, but she looked awful. Had she been crying? I decided to say something: "Mom, I'm worried. I think . . . well . . . you look depressed."

27

"I'm not depressed."

"Look at your eyes. They're all red."

"I'm chopping scallions, Lisa, for heaven's sake."

"Oh. Well, I didn't mean only now."

"Lisa, I know you mean well, but please stop watching me. I don't need to be studied by you. I'm not one of your spiders. Please. I'm still your mother; you're still my daughter—I hope—so stop trying to take over."

"I'm not trying to take over. I *care* about you, Mom!"

"I know you do. I care about you, too. Now, please . . . everything is fine. Stop worrying. Okay? Lisa?"

"Okay. Okay. Mother knows best. Right?" I wondered if Mother did.

"Right," she said.

"I'll finish the Cantonese shrimp."

"You can get it all ready, but you have to wait—"

"I know, Mom. We've made it before. It has to be cooked at the last minute."

"See, you're learning. I'm going to get into my leotards. . . . Thank you, Lisa. For caring."

"Oh, bull."

She took her martini glass with her as she headed for the stairway.

"Mom! Drinking depresses people."

28

"This is only melted ice," she said, swirling her glass.

Beautiful! Well, I'd tried. I tackled the mess of raw shrimp, first removing the shells, then the veins or intestines or ripcords or whatever they were. As I worked, the neatness factor in the kitchen dropped rapidly. I poured some oil into the big pan that served as a wok and started adding the chopped scallions and ground pork. What was bothering Mom, I wondered. I was sure something was. Was it her super-sloppy daughter? Was it Dad? Was Dad possibly fooling around with someone else? Was *she* fooling around with someone else? Mom and Dad didn't seem to spend much time together anymore, just the two of them; they always had to be with other people. Maybe I was reading too much into things, the way Kim does. But this was one of those many moments when I wished I had a sister or brother to talk to.

I'd gotten everything ready for dinner, to the point of actual cooking, including the rice and the egg-drop soup, and had cleaned up and set the table with our Chinese plates and little bowls and teacups. And chopsticks. Chinese food really tastes better with chopsticks, once you learn how to use them.

Dad still wasn't home, so I went up to the bathroom that he'd converted into a darkroom. I like being there;

29

in a lot of ways it's my favorite place in the house. It's one of the only *real* places in the house, I can tell you that. I love everything in that room: the bottles of chemicals on the shelves, the enlarger on its heavy frame looking like a sci-fi robot, the printing easel, the developing tanks and reels, the sets of trays, everything. When I'm working there, the rest of the world disappears. Sometimes even *I* disappear. In the darkroom, when my prints are coming out right, I become Dorothea Lange for a while. Bull, right? But that's how I feel.

I sat on the closed toilet seat and studied my latest contact prints. Pretty awful, more Lisa Daniels than Lange. I hadn't bracketed my exposures properly. I'd been at least one stop off, f/16 instead of f/11, underexposing the whole roll. There just wasn't enough contrast; everything seemed gray. And grainy.

It was supposed to have been a photo series about the stores along our main street in Lake Hills; shots of the nice, shiny glass fronts, and, paired with those, the ugly backs of the same stores, garbage pails and all. Like seeing Hollywood stars in hair curlers. I'd gotten the idea from something I'd seen in a Soho art gallery in New York a couple of weeks ago, when I'd gone into the city with Mom and Dad. Only that had been a photo series showing the fronts and backs of famous paintings. The backs were just canvas, wood frames, and supports. I'd gotten an eerie feeling of the fabricatedness, if there's such a word, of the paintings. The paintings began to feel like stage props; you lost your belief in them. Well, that's what I wanted to try with the stores.

My prints weren't a total loss; I saw a lot of things I could do to make the series more interesting. I decided I'd try again, and maybe enter the series in the contest as a photo essay on glitz versus reality.

I noticed Dad standing outside the door to the darkroom, watching me. He does that every so often, just comes into the house quietly without anyone knowing. When I come home, it's like the circus has come to town.

"Hi," I said, tossing the contact prints down. I was supposed to start the shrimp the moment he came in.

"Hi, sweets," he said.

"Hi, sour," I answered. I've asked him not to call me "sweets," but he keeps doing it from habit, I guess. I've told him if he does, I'll call him sour. Except, I think he likes it; so I'm thinking of switching to calling him Herbert. Dad definitely dislikes kids calling their parents by their first names.

"I saw those new photos last night," he said, nodding toward the prints. "What in the dickens are they supposed to be?''

"Can't you tell? It's Main Street from front and rear.''

"But that's at least ten bucks worth of film and paper. Why do it? I don't understand, sweets. I really don't.''

"Well, Herbert, it's—''

"Well, *what*?''

"Uh . . . Herbert,'' I said, wavering. "Dad, please don't call me sweets. I'm not three years old. Anyway, this is a study. It's—remember those pictures we saw in Soho? The backs of paintings? It's like those.''

"Well, it's your money, swee—Lisa. Where's Mom hiding?''

"She's getting ready for her dance group. Dad, I— I don't know. I'm worried maybe Mom's drinking too much.''

"Come on. Don't be silly.''

"She is. And she looks so depressed. Haven't you noticed how down she is sometimes?''

"It'll pass, Lisa. Everyone has problems: Mom and I aren't exceptions. We're human, I think.''

"You guys have been fighting a lot, too.''

"We're human, Lisa. Just human.''

"Dad, please. Can't you tell me what's going on?''

"I don't really know. Mom's a perfectionist, for one

32

thing. You know that. And I'm not perfect."

"Neither am I! What's going on?"

"And we're not getting any younger. Things start catching up with you."

"Dad. Please. Talk! You don't have to do a Madison Avenue story-board routine with me."

"Lisa, there's nothing to tell. Don't make this into a two-hour prime-time special. There's nothing for you to worry about. Believe me. Okay, sweets?"

"That's what Mom said. Okay, Herbie."

"Herbie, eh? There go your darkroom privileges for the next ten years."

4

I BARELY SPOKE to Kim before science class the next morning, just enough to say I didn't think I'd be able to have lunch with her that day. She didn't seem to realize that anything was wrong, and I decided to cool it and not have a big confrontation. I almost liked the fact that she was so oblivious to things. I guess she hadn't meant to hurt me yesterday.

Adam scarcely glanced at me in science; he was too busy studying an astronomy book he'd brought to school. It's a good thing Mrs. Smile-Awhile Felts didn't call on him. I was convinced that he'd forgotten all about our meeting at two-thirty, and I decided I wouldn't remind him. Go-with-the-flow, that's my middle name.

But at half-past two, there he was at the front entrance, juggling his load of books. Why didn't he use a backpack like everyone else?

"Hi," I said.

"H-h-hi."

It was strange; I liked his stutter. It made him seem vulnerable. I got on his bus instead of mine and found a free seat across the aisle, two rows behind him. The kids seated near him began fooling around with one another, as if he were an inanimate object in their way, kind of trying to harass him. Adam didn't seem to notice; he just stared down at his lap as the bus wound up Blue Spring Road into the hilly area. Then one guy pretended to hit him with a book. Adam still didn't look up, though his shoulders tensed. Was it self-defense or total withdrawal, I wondered. Maybe both at once.

Right before his stop Adam turned toward me and nodded. Mom always signals me like that when we're separated on a crowded bus in New York. I scrambled off right behind him. Since we were the only ones getting off, and I didn't belong on that bus, half the kids started going *Whooo!* Talk about absolute gross. I turned back toward the bus, stuck out my tongue, and wiggled my hands up at my ears, like a little kid. I was really angry, but everybody applauded. Adam didn't seem to have the foggiest idea of what was going on.

We started walking up a dirt road toward a big old house at the end. It must have been built around the turn of the century. I'd seen houses like that down at Cape May, on the southern tip of New Jersey. I wished I had my camera; I would have loved to take some shots of that porch with all the filigreed wood and gingerbread everywhere. Only it wasn't Adam's house. About a hundred feet before it, he suddenly started going up a steep narrow path into the woods. He couldn't live up *there*! Where was he leading me? Kim's warning came back to me in neon lights.

What to do? I stopped dead in my tracks while Adam continued a short way up the path, no doubt thinking I was behind him. After a moment he came back.

"We have to go this way. I live up th-there."

"Adam, you know, maybe this wasn't such a great idea. You know? I, uh—I'm really supposed to be home by four. Look, I believe you about the capsule."

"N-no, you don't."

He looked hurt. Could he know what I was thinking? Headlines were zipping through my brain about Lisa Daniels, found in the woods, her blood-soaked clothing hanging from every branch. Adam was standing there with his load of books under one arm, waiting for me.

"Adam, I really ought to go."

"Come on up with me. Please. I w-want you to see it."

"I don't know." I was weakening. His *please* was so begging it was painful.

"I w-want you to see it. Please," he said again.

"Why? Why me?"

"Because you t-talked to me in science and the library and you didn't laugh at me."

"*Nobody's* laughing at you!" I said.

"Yes, they are. . . . They are. . . ."

"So what! Let them! Who gives a damn! They laugh at me, too!"

"Let's go up. Please? Don't worry, I really live up there. I'm not going to h-hurt you or anything. . . ."

He *did* know what was bothering me. Well, the hell with Kim's warnings. "Okay," I said.

"Okay!" he said, brightening. "Come on! Follow me. It's a short cut."

We walked and walked. And walked. If this was the short cut, I wondered what the long cut was like. I never knew we had hills this high in our part of New Jersey. It seemed like we were going up a small mountain. Finally, we reached a clearing where the terrain

37

flattened out. There was a big pond, or, I should say, a small lake surrounded by trees: oaks, maples, and a stand of fir trees. It was beautiful.

"Th-that's where I swim," said Adam. "It's an old surface mine. Iron. It's very deep. I have to swim a lot because it's like—I have to be underwater a lot. So when I go back, I can live there again."

"You mean on Vega-X?" Where does imagination end and craziness begin, I wondered.

"We live underwater there."

"I know; you told me something like that."

"Come on," he said. "I'll show you. Want to swim?"

"Good grief! Thanks! No thanks!" It was only mid-May and that pond looked frigid. But that wasn't going to stop Adam. He took off his shirt, leaving just his T-shirt, torn I might add. Then he took off his shoes and socks, emptied his pockets, and plunged in. *Kapow!*

It was wild! One second Adam Bates was standing on the shore; the next second he was gone. I mean *gone!* Nothing. A lot of bubbles where he'd jumped in, and nothing else. The surface was smooth as glass. Could he have gotten hurt?

I waited ten seconds, then went over to the edge and looked down. Zero. No bottom. It must have been very deep, even at the edge. I guess old mine shafts would be.

"Adam!" I called, feeling uneasy. It must have been twenty seconds now, and I was really worried. I assumed he knew what he was doing, but then again, maybe he didn't. Maybe he was showing off. Or really believed he could live without air. *What do I do?* flashed through my mind. I could swim, but not well. I started calling, embarrassed, but scared.

"Help! Someone!"

Nothing. It was over half a minute. I took my shoes and socks off, whatever good that would do. I could swim on the surface, but I couldn't dive more than four or five feet.

"HELP! SOMEONE! PLEASE HELP! HELP!"

It was forty seconds. He must be drowning. He must be dead.

"HELP! OH, PLEASE! HELP! HELP!"

There was a crash at the far end of the lake and Adam shot up out of the water and screamed, "*Ya-hooo!*"

I was on the ground, squatting, feeling weak all over. "*Yoww!*" he shouted and plunged down in again. How could he do it? I put one bare foot gingerly into the water at the edge; it was ice. This time he was under for fifty-three seconds by my watch. I wasn't worried now, just absolutely amazed. I was beginning to wonder whether there really *was* a planet Vega-X.

There was another huge explosion of water, and

Adam was up on the shore next to me. He wasn't even out of breath. His T-shirt and jeans clung to his body, and I must say, he looked sort of sexy even though he didn't have Russ's muscle-man build.

"H-how's that? That's how we live out there." He nodded toward the sky above the treeline.

"Aren't you cold?"

"Me? No."

"But you could catch pneumonia! Your clothes are soaked!"

"I'm okay. If you weren't here, I'd have s-swum naked."

"Go ahead. Don't mind me," I said. That *would* have been interesting.

"Okay. Here goes." He started to take off his jeans. He was a nut! Maybe I did need my danger whistle!

"No!" I called out.

"You s-said go ahead."

"I was kidding. Don't!"

"Why not?"

"Oh, come on, Adam! Because it would be, well, embarrassing. For me, at least."

"Okay. Some other time."

"Right. Some other time."

Adam got his shoes and socks back on, and we continued along the path for another five minutes. There was nothing around. I could have shouted for help back at the lake all day; nobody would have heard.

"You know," I said as we walked, "you really ought to go out for the swim team. That was some swimming you just did."

"No. I just s-swim for myself."

"But you're fantastic."

"No, I'm not." He looked at me shyly, then looked away, shrugging. So different from Russ, the macho king.

We came to a dirt road with deep tire ruts in it. Adam turned onto the road and we walked between the ruts.

"We could have come this w-way," he said. "But you've got to walk twice as far."

After a few more minutes, I spotted what looked like a big abandoned shack in the distance. There was a rusted-out truck and what must have been some old chicken coops. Then it dawned on me. Years ago, Grandpa had told me about the hill people who lived in the northwestern part of New Jersey. Many had worked in the old iron mines, until they finally shut the mines down. He'd said some of these people were a hundred years behind the times and never registered to vote or anything, and even had feuds like in Kentucky.

41

As we got closer I saw a girl of seven or eight playing in front of one of the coops.

"Adam!" she called down the road.

"Hey, Emily!" Adam shouted back. She came running to meet us.

"Adam, I got the eggs!"

"You got all the eggs? Hey, g-good, Emily." Adam put his books down, then lifted Emily up and swung her around three or four times in a wide circle. She screamed with happiness. Then he put her down in front of me.

"This is my sister, Emily. Emily, this is L-l-lisa."

"Hello," I said. "Hi, Emily."

"Hi. Are you Adam's friend?"

"Yes," I said.

A woman's voice from the house called, "Emily!" Emily looked at me, then toward the house, then back at me, not wanting to go. "Emily!" the woman called again.

Emily turned and ran toward the house, stopped and looked back at me, then turned and ran, once more.

"That's my m-mother calling," said Adam. "That's my house over there."

What could I say? The house was dilapidated and falling apart. There was almost no paint left on it, and there were sheet-metal patches all over the roof. The yard was full of all kinds of junk: old rusty tricycles, an old shovel, an abandoned boiler, some huge tires off that rusted truck, you name it.

"Your house is *really* far away from everything, isn't it," I said.

"This isn't my house."

"But, I thought you just said—"

"This is where I'm supposed to s-stay. They assigned it to me, back on Vega-X. I have to stay here awhile. So I can learn."

"Oh." He brought it into everything, the way Kim connects sex with everything. That's what being obsessed is, I guess. "Well, anyway, I like your sister," I said.

"I like Emily, too," he said. "I w-wish she really *was* my sister. But she isn't. And my mother isn't really my mother. She doesn't understand. I explained it, b-but she doesn't understand."

"How about your father?"

"He's gone. But he's not my f-father, either. He thinks he is, but he's wrong."

Could he possibly have been adopted, I wondered. Or was this just another part of his fantasy. We walked over to the house, and I must say, I was a little uptight about going inside. But it wasn't bad at all; in fact, it was kind of nice; cool and damp. Then I realized with

43

a jolt that there was no floor. The floor was hard-packed dirt. Pretty incredible. How poor can you get? I thought for a moment of the families in the West Dorothea Lange had photographed many years ago. This didn't seem all that different.

But there was a smell of something baking, and that gave a glow to everything. We came into a big main room. There was an old table and some chairs and something that looked like a wooden icebox. And there was a beautiful big clock with a pendulum. They even had pictures on the unpainted wooden walls, including one of the astronauts landing on the moon, of all things. Adam must have put that up. The only modern thing they had was a TV in one corner.

It was like being in an old run-down antique shop. I looked around shamelessly. There seemed to be two categories of stuff. There were old beat-up things like the rickety brass bed in the adjoining room where I assumed Adam's mother slept. And there were some beautiful things like that clock, and that old icebox, and a wooden chest with black metal bands around it, things that the family must have saved from long ago. And there was a huge fireplace that seemed to serve two rooms, this room and the room behind it.

"I like your house," I said to Adam, and it was true. Again, I wished I had my camera. Maybe the house was shabby and falling apart, but there wasn't one phony thing anywhere. The bedroom was a bedroom, not a boudoir like the master bedroom in our house. When Adam opened the antique icebox to get some milk, I saw that it really was an icebox, and not converted to a plant holder or record cabinet. And when I looked outside in the yard, I could see Emily climbing in and out of the stacks of old tires. It wasn't just junk I saw; it was a playground.

Adam's mother—if she was his mother—came into the big room from the kitchen. She was a large, plain, pleasant-looking woman. She was wearing a house-dress one size too small, the way my grandmother used to do. I liked her even before she spoke.

"Oh. You're Lisa!" she said in a loud, firm voice. Adam had prepared her.

"Yeah. Hi," I said, in my always elegant way.

"Well! Hello! Now, Adam, you didn't go and give Lisa milk without my hot muffins, did you? Now, Lisa! You have to have some muffins if you want to be my friend! They're hot, so the butter and honey will melt right in!"

"Oh, they smell wonderful. Thank you," I said meekly. I bit into one of the muffins with butter and honey oozing, and it was sheer heaven. I had the quick funny feeling of realizing that, just as the furniture might have been used exactly like this a hundred years ago, these muffins had probably been made exactly like this back then. It was like stepping back into American hist—

And I knew it. I didn't think it; I *knew* it. This, *this* was my photo essay. This house, these people, the whole thing. Oh, it would be unbelievable! It was precisely the sort of photos that Walker Evans and Dorothea Lange, my Dorothea, had taken during the Depression. I walked into the kitchen and it was great. The oven where the muffins were being baked burned wood. And you pumped water directly into the sink with a big handle, from a well below. There were metal cake and cookie molds hanging from hooks on the wall, and pots and pans black from fires, real fires, not gas or electric stoves. And there was a huge old cupboard with broken glass doors full of a million mismatched cups and saucers and plates and bowls. The more I saw of the house, the more I liked it.

Emily came in to claim a muffin. "My turn," she said, trying to get one out of the oven.

"Oh, Emily!" Mrs. Bates said in her big voice. "You'll burn yourself, good and proper! Oh, look at those hands! Go to the sink, quick now, and I'll get you the biggest, fattest muffin of them all!" Then Mrs. Bates turned toward me. "She's the sweetest girl! The

46

sweetest girl! She's so good in arithmetic! Just like Adam. But she's not reading too good, they said at school. So I said to them, I said, 'Well! Some folks read real good. And other folks *are* real good. You give me the choice, I'll take *are* over *read*, any day of the week!' And that shut them up! You should have seen them . . . Here's your muffin, Emily, baby.''

Oh, wow! I'll bet Mrs. Bates doesn't need a martini every day to keep her going. And she's probably got a lot more problems than Mom.

Adam had gone to a small room near the kitchen, his room, I guessed, to put on some dry clothes. As I ate my muffin, Emily came over to the table and offered me hers.

"No thanks, Emily," I said. "I have my own."

"Mine's better," she said. She actually seemed hurt.

"Well, a little piece." I broke off a small part of her muffin and ate it. Emily giggled with happiness. "I see what you mean about real good," I said to Mrs. Bates.

"We've had our troubles," she answered. "But Emily's sure not one of them."

Adam had come back wearing another pair of ripped jeans. He plucked a muffin out of the oven, barehanded.

"Adam, you'll burn yourself to death!" said Mrs. Bates.

"Not me. I told you before; fire is eight times hotter on Vega-X."

"Oh, sure!" boomed Mrs. Bates. "And the moon is made of Swiss cheese."

Well she knew about it, just as Adam had said. But she obviously didn't believe it.

I could see that Adam was annoyed with her answer. He looked down at the dirt floor and started scuffing it with his shoe. "Come on, L-lisa," he said. "I'll show you that thing, like I promised."

"What thing?" Mrs. Bates asked.

"Nothing," said Adam.

"Nothing is nothing! But I know. Now you have a girlfriend, you can keep secrets from your Ma. You got someone else for secrets. Just teasing, Lisa! Don't take me serious, honey. I'm a teaser!"

Well . . . but it *was* embarrassing. To say the least. Maybe nobody can be a hundred percent, including warm, generous early-American mothers. Score one for my own mother; Mom would never have said something like that in front of Adam. I hope. But you can bet she would have thought it.

"Hey, Ma," said Adam. "She isn't my g-girl-friend."

It was getting worse. Were they going to have a debate about me? Maybe I could be the referee.

"Oh, Adam!" his mother said. "Go on now! You never brought a girl back here before!"

Worse and worse. She spoke as if I wasn't there. I said very quickly, "I just came to see Adam's capsule."

"Well, I don't know what capsule you're talking about, honey. We don't have no capsules."

Emily joined in. "Space capsule," she said.

"Oh, not *that*! Adam, are you going to show her that piece of junk?"

Adam's face turned red, but he talked very softly so as not to lose his temper, I guessed. I could see him struggling with it. "It isn't junk, Ma. You d-don't understand."

"I do too understand. Don't I, Emily!"

"Come on, L-lisa. Let's go. Are you coming?" He was on his way out the door, and I had to do a sort of pirouette to follow him and yet say thank you to his mother for the muffin and everything.

"You're welcome, honey. Come any time. Do you like chicken with nice sweet dumplings? Well, that's one of my specials. I hate sewing and fixing, but, honey, I love to cook. You come for dinner soon now."

"Thank you. Thanks a lot." She certainly was warm and friendly, though I guess I pulled away a little when she stopped me and planted a huge kiss on my cheek.

49

Good grief. She was acting as if I was her daughter-in-law or something.

There was more discarded stuff in the backyard: part of an old tractor, a roll of wire fence, more old tires, an oil drum, and lots of wreckage I couldn't quite figure out. I would have loved to poke around, but Adam was walking at top speed toward the woods that stretched farther up the hill beyond the cleared area.

"D-don't let my mother bother you," said Adam, as I half-jogged beside him. "She doesn't understand. She's okay."

"Oh, I like her," I said.

"She's not really my m-mother, but she's okay."

There was a small wooden structure with a single door on it, to our right. "What's that, Adam?" I brilliantly asked.

"That's the outhouse. We don't have a toilet."

I should have known; I could smell it now. How could I be so dumb? I guess I never dreamed that anybody in New Jersey used outhouses anymore.

"Oh, of course," I said, recovering my cool as best I could. "It's very nice—uh—interesting—uh . . ."

For the first time Adam showed some glimmer of humor. "It's my home away from h-home."

"It must be freezing in the winter," I said, getting down to the nitty-gritty photojournalist facts.

"It is. But we got a c-chemical toilet from welfare, for inside the house. Anyway, they're trying to evict us—the county. They say it's unsanitary and we don't have enough heat and a m-million other things. They're trying to move us to a trailer park. But Ma won't let them."

"Why not? It must be hard, living like this."

"Yeah. But Ma says her f-family goes back over two hundred years in these hills. From before the Revolution. And she says she won't move, even though they've moved most of the other people."

"But, still, it must be hard," I said. This *had* to be my photo essay; it sounded as if there wouldn't be any families like Adam's left in these hills soon. It would all disappear, forever.

I hoped he would tell me more as we walked. But all he said was, "That's why they sent me here. Because it's hard. Th-that way, you learn more." It was back to the Vega-X story, as usual.

Maybe the best thing was to relax and act like his mother about it, and not pay too much attention. Of course, if there *was* a real space capsule . . . What then? For one thing, we'd all be very famous, very fast. Because if it really was true, I'd be back with all my cameras before you could say *exclusive scoop!*

51

5

WE WALKED THROUGH the woods. There were pine trees, and the narrow path was soft and spongy with last year's bed of needles. With the sun coming down in slanting layers, and the birds, and the clean smell of pine, it was magic, like entering a Disney kingdom.

"I l-like to come up here and sit very quietly," said Adam. "I just sit and listen. We don't have this on Vega-X."

"We don't have this on earth much, either," I said.

We must have been walking for ten minutes, always uphill, when we came to a knoll, sort of a hill on top of the hill. There were trees all around us, but the knoll was clear. We climbed to the top along a pebbly path, single file. From the highest point I could see Adam's house and a few other houses scattered here and there in the woods below. And farther off in the distance, I saw the road the school bus had followed, and beyond, in the haze, the tiny buildings of Lake Hills. I tried to locate my own house, but I couldn't.

"Some view!" I said. "Fantastic!"

"I guess that's why they landed here," said Adam. "So they could see anybody coming."

"Who?" I asked, as if I didn't know by now.

"The ones that b-brought me here. They must have come in their own capsules, just like mine. But they went back."

"Okay, Adam, baby! Put up or shut up! Where's this famous space capsule?"

He motioned me to follow him down the other side of the knoll into a half-wooded area. Some old fallen trees were caught on other trees at crazy angles to the ground. One of them hung like a huge cannon pointed at thirty degrees toward the sun.

"I figure the c-capsules knocked these trees down with their rocket blast," Adam said.

"Mm-hmm," I murmured skeptically. Yet the trees did seem to have fallen outwardly, like spokes around

53

a central hub. The hub was a huge mound of pinecones and broken evergreen branches and debris; it reminded me of a pile of discarded Christmas trees. Adam started lifting the branches off the pile and placing them to the side. I helped him, and after a few minutes, I saw a glint of metal underneath. There was something there, all right.

As we pulled more branches off, I could see parts of an enormous copper-colored hemisphere sticking out of the ground. There was a hole in the surface, near the top. The metal dome did look a little like the reentry capsules the astronauts used when they'd returned to earth from their lunar landings years ago. I got a chilly feeling. . . . Could it be? Could there be something to Adam's story, after all?

"I hid it," Adam said, as he cleared more branches away. "I don't want anybody b-but Ma and Emily to see it."

"Well, but I'm seeing it."

"And you."

I felt a mixture of pride that he trusted me, and worry that he was liking me more than I ought to let him like me, unless I really liked him quite a lot, which I wasn't totally sure about. I know that's confusing, but that's how I felt at the moment.

"It really is something," I said. Most of the big

sphere or capsule was still buried in the ground. Part of the exposed surface was covered with a greenish coating, as if it was corroding, but other parts had been cleaned and polished, by Adam, I assumed.

"I haven't dug it all out yet," said Adam. "It's in there very deep."

"But it could be anything," I said, not giving in. "It could be—I don't know—just a huge old boiler or water tank."

"But why would anyone b-bury a boiler all the way up here? They'd be crazy to carry it all the way up here. And boilers don't look like this. There's an old one in our yard. Boilers are c-cylindrical. This is all round and smooth and beautiful."

He was right. I couldn't argue with that. It was beautiful. The polished surfaces shone in the sun like convex mirrors, and the capsule was perfectly round, like a half globe. Up there in the woods with nothing but trees and wild ferns around, I felt as if I was in a science-fiction movie.

"Well, it's unusual, I've got to admit," I said. "But it doesn't mean it's a space capsule." I don't throw in the towel easily.

"It's a space capsule all right," he said. "I don't care if you don't b-believe me. I know what I know. I get these dreams. They send me dreams at night. And

55

I dreamed I was here; there were people standing around, and I was inside the capsule, and I was just a little kid. Up here. So I came up last year with Emily and dug and there it was. I swear. I dreamed it, then I f-found it right where it was in my dream.''

"Wow," I said. "That's really spooky.''

"No. It's just what happened, that's all.''

There had been a program on TV last month about ESP, extrasensory perception, and some scientists thought it may actually exist. So why couldn't Adam be right about their communicating with him through dreams? Maybe the whole thing was true. Maybe some-day the whole world would say this was it! The break-through! Someone from another planet! It could be the story of the century. Or so I thought at the moment.

But, of course, the sensible part of me knew that it was all baloney. Let's face it, if Adam had come from some faraway planet, he'd probably look like a giant mushroom, or a pink caterpillar, rather than a not-bad-looking teenager.

Still, there really *was* something there. If I'd had that dream and then dug and found a capsule, I would have gone to the library and done some research to try to figure it out, just as Adam had. Only I wouldn't have made up a planet Vega-X with no oxygen, and all that. I'm very matter-of-fact. I guess I would have

56

asked Mom and Dad to get an expert to come and examine the capsule.

But there *was* something there. Score one for Adam. If it wasn't a space capsule, it certainly was unusual. I was glad. He wasn't really bats. He was probably just overdosing on science-fiction daydreams.

"I'm impressed," I said. "Really. I don't know what it all means, but I'm impressed. I could help you dig it out more if you want."

"It's hard. There's big rocks."

"We could try."

"I tried. It's very hard."

I wondered if he actually didn't want to dig it out. Maybe he was afraid it might wreck his story, depending on what he found.

"Say, Adam, did you ever think of getting an expert from, say, NASA to look at it?"

"No! I don't need an expert! If they came, this hill would be c-covered with TV cameras. Don't you tell anybody, Lisa! Please!"

"Oh, I won't. Don't worry."

He started putting the pine branches back over the hemisphere, and I helped him. It didn't seem necessary; I couldn't see how anyone would ever find this spot up here, even if they tried. I was sure I couldn't.

As we were walking back down to his house, Adam's

hand brushed mine, by accident, I think. But he pulled back as if it had been an electric shock. So I swung my hand and slapped his, playfully. He pulled back, so I did it again, and again, he pulled away.

"People don't t-t-touch on Vega-X," he said. And I'd thought I'd be in mortal danger, alone with him in the woods.

"Oh really," I said. "Well they do on Earth-X!" And I slapped his hand once more. This time, he let me.

As we reached his house, Emily rushed over. "Did you see it?" she asked me. "I've been polishing it."

"I could tell," I said. "It's beautiful."

"Come on, Emily," Adam said. "One ride!"

He took her by both hands and started to swing her around and around, as he'd done before. Emily loved it. She screamed, "More! More!"

Again, I wished I had my camera. I wondered if this was a good time to ask Adam if I could take some photos of his house and everything, for my essay. But I decided I'd better wait; instead, I invited him to come over my house tomorrow and see my photographs. I figured he'd understand better when he saw what I did. I know: inviting him over seemed to say pretty loudly *I like you*. Well, I did like him.

He seemed really thrown about being asked to come over. "Y-your house?"

"Sure. I'll make some popcorn. And you can see my masterpieces."

"You want me to c-come to your house?"

"Yes."

"I can't."

"Why not?"

"I—I don't know. . . . Y-your house?" He looked scared. I don't think he'd been invited to anyone's house in his life.

"Hey, come on. You invited me here, right? Now I'm inviting you to see my incredible photos. Okay?"

"Okay . . . I'll come!" he said, as if he'd made a momentous decision.

"Good. Front of the school at two-thirty, just like today. Okay?"

"Okay."

"I guess I'd better be going," I said. "Is there a bus that goes back to town along the road down below?"

"I don't think so."

"Whoops! I guess I should have taken my bike."

"You can use my b-bike," said Adam.

"Okay. Terrific."

He brought out this rusty bike from the woodshed at the side of the house. It must have been fifty years old, with big heavy handlebars and coaster brakes. But it worked. He helped me take it down through the woods, half carrying and half riding it, bouncing over all the ruts. Then he set the bike on the road for me and stood there awkwardly.

"Lisa, I—uh . . . I . . ." He shrugged, reached toward my hand, then stopped and shook his head.

"What?"

"Well, you know . . . on Vega-X, like I said, people don't t-touch." There was a huge gap in his logic, because he certainly touched Emily when he swung her around. But I didn't want to pursue that.

"Vega-X sounds like a pretty dull place," I said as I reached out and squeezed his hand. It wasn't exactly a handshake, which would have been dumb; it was more an I-like-you-enough-so-that-when-we-say-good-bye-I-want-to-touch-you-in-some-way-but-not-too-much-and-not-too-little sort of thing. Whatever *that* is. Which I think is what he wanted to do in the first place. Anyway, he squeezed back, hard. Good. "See what I mean? Much duller than planet Earth, right?" I said. "You're lucky you're here."

"N-no, I'm not," he said, as he released my hand. "I don't want to be here."

"Why not?"

"People hurt people here. A lot. A lot." His face looked awful, as if someone was hurting him right then and there.

60

"I, uh—Adam, am *I* hurting you?"

"No. Not you . . . Tomorrow? I'll see you tomorrow?"

"Sure. You bet."

"Okay. Tomorrow," he said, and turned and ran back up into the woods.

6

KIM AND I started speaking to each other again that next morning in the girls' locker room. To be exact, she never stopped talking to me, it's rather that I'd practically stopped talking to her. But I could not *not* tell her about Adam coming to my house that afternoon. Or about my mother's sarcastic remark at breakfast. "A *boy* is coming here?" she'd asked with feigned disbelief.

"Yes, Mother. A *boy*!"

"Well, it's about time." *Whammo!* Right between the eyes.

62

But I took care of Mom. "He's twenty-two, Mom, and we're going to drive into New York after, to go slam-dancing in the Village."

"What! Twenty-two!"

That woke her up. Once I explained that I was jesting—that was the word I used: jesting—she grew positively buoyant. At last her misfit daughter, Lisa the Loner, the Camera Kook, had a boyfriend! Or so she wished to think. I was more than a little concerned with how buoyant she'd be after she met Adam, with his ripped jeans and his planet Vega address. Or, for that matter, his planet Earth address. I think Mom had someone like Joshua Freeman down the block in mind for me. He's some kind of super genius and is probably going to become a neurosurgeon, or a psychiatrist. Of course he's already got a girlfriend, but that doesn't stop Mom. She and Mrs. Freeman are in the same dance group, which makes Mom think one thing could lead to another.

I told Kim the news while we were changing for gym class. The locker room was total chaos as usual, heightened by a leaky water pipe in the ceiling that had created a small lake around half of the lockers, crowding us all toward the other half. I had to shout.

"He's wild, Kim!" Did I subconsciously want everyone to hear, to show the world that I, too, was boyfriended now? I couldn't stop; I was on a roll. "He wanted to swim in the nude!" Heads turned. Many heads. They didn't know I was referring to Adam; only Kim knew. Did that make it all right? All I know is that I enjoyed the attention thoroughly.

"I *told* you!" said Kim. "Didn't I?"

"Oh, no, no. It was no problem. It was all very friendly." The heads were still turned and were drawing closer, like those ads on TV where everybody listens when somebody who knows about the stock market talks. It was bad. Have you ever suddenly seen that what you're doing is actually an imitation of your mother or father? Well I saw as clear as day that I was imitating Mom when she's slightly crocked at a party. I was showing off and exaggerating.

"Well, what did you do?" Kim asked. Two dozen ears were listening now.

"I'll tell you later." I wasn't going to announce to my audience that I'd done absolutely nothing. Talk about boys bragging in the locker room; I was just as bad. As I think back, I'm embarrassed about that whole scene.

"I can't believe it. You really like him, don't you," said Kim. She was beginning to rub a raw nerve again.

"Yes, I do! Not everybody has to be like Russ!"

"Okay! Big deal!"

"He's quite a person!" I continued, pretty aggressively. I was regretting that stupid remark I'd made about swimming in the buff; all it had done was confirm Kim's feelings about Adam.

"It's none of my business," said Kim.

"You bet it isn't!"

"You don't have to get sore!"

"I'm not sore!"

"Okay!"

"Okay!"

We had both changed by now and were ready to go into the gym. I was feeling miserable all over again, arguing with Kim. "Kim, he's nice," I said, almost begging for her approval. "He gave me his bike to ride home. And he's really bright. And, well, he's nice." But I couldn't tell her anything about Vega-X, so it was only half the story. The good half.

Kim looked me right in the eye, eyeball to eyeball, and said, "I hope you're right. Because I don't want you to get all messed up. See, it *is* my business. Because you're my friend, and I love you. You dope."

Well, folks, I, Lisa Daniels, hard-headed photojournalist, got a sudden pair of slightly wet eyes. Good old Kim. She really did care. I had to be dense not to see it.

Adam slipped me a note in science. Lo and behold, the note was wrapped around a flower, a wilted iris.

The note said: *I'll meet you at two-thirty. This is for you. Sincerely. Your friend. Adam.*

Oh. Just *oh!* I loved it. The note. The flower. The awkwardness. The works. If Adam Bates had gotten the world's ten greatest experts on romance and courtship to advise him on how to win the heart of Miss Lisa D., they couldn't have come up with anything better than this.

But I wondered, again, whether he was liking me too much, too fast. It reminded me of how, when I walk with someone taller or faster than me—Dad, for instance—I have to do a little running step every so often, to keep up. I liked Adam, but I felt he was getting ahead of me.

Still, it was nice. *He* was nice. Had Kim seen the flower? No. I slipped it into my backpack. I'd never hear the end of it; I'd convinced Kim and my mother that I hated flowers, real or photographed.

This definitely seemed to be one of my days. Every class went like a breeze, with a flower in my backpack and a song in my heart. Definitely my day, until Adam and I got to my house after school, that is.

Mom was waiting right at the door, and she seemed depressed again. Why? She'd been fine at breakfast when I'd made my announcement about Adam coming over. She'd seemed really happy for once. But now she had a martini glass in her hand and she seemed a little sloshed. Was she depressed because of the martini, or had she mixed herself a martini because she was depressed? I couldn't say; all I knew was that this was some way to meet your daughter's friend.

"Mom, uh, this is Adam," I said, with overtones of doom. "Adam, this is, uh, Mom."

"Hello. Adam?" She was trying to be relaxed and was working hard at it, I could see. "How very, very nice. Lisa didn't tell me that you were so, well, so good-look—" Mom caught my icy stare. In a faint, fading voice she said, "Attractive . . . Well! Come in, Adam! And make yourself at home. . . . Would you care for some, um, soda?"

"N-n-no thanks." Yes, Mother, he has a stammer. No, Mother, it doesn't mean he's an idiot. Had she noticed his jeans yet? No, I didn't think so. Maybe I should have warned her ahead of time. But I hadn't. Dumb of me.

Adam took a few steps into our living room, then stopped. The room is huge. There's a fireplace along one wall, with a raised hearth, and the wall has gray bricks from floor to ceiling. And there's an enormous glass and steel coffee table. And there are those glass cabinets, with Mom's prize collection of paperweights and rare seashells. And an inch-thick carpet.

You get the picture. Adam seemed afraid to move, or even breathe.

"Soda? Or milk?" Mom asked again.

"Mom, we're fine!" I said, begging her with my eyes to leave. But no, she came around behind me and put her hands on my shoulders, turning us into a living monument dedicated to blissful mother-and-daughterhood. Pals to the end. She was really looking at Adam now. Staring would be a better word.

"Say, Adam, would you like me to put on some music?" I asked, nervously, as I tried to wriggle free from Mom. "Do you like the Police?"

"Uh—uh—I d-don't know. I d-don't need any m-music," Adam stammered, obviously made super tense by Mom's just standing there, and by our huge, glitzy zoo of a living room. He looked around the room, evading Mom's eyes, and studied the glass paperweights, Mom's pride and joy. These paperweights are the kind that have flowers or butterflies or designs embedded deep in the glass. They shone in pinpoints of light. Mom normally never turned those lights on except for her own guests at night.

"W-what's those things?" asked Adam. He shouldn't have asked. I could read Mom's mind; you're supposed to know what they are, if you're civilized, that is. Worse, he was picking one up. Worse yet, the rip in his jeans was now gloriously visible.

"Oh!" Mom called out, reaching toward the paperweight, protectively. "Those are antiques! They're antique paperweights. Please be very careful. Please."

Then Mom whispered in my ear, and I prayed that Adam couldn't hear. "Lisa—he seems very odd. Something's wrong with him!"

"Mom, he's okay," I whispered back through gritted teeth. "Please leave us alone!"

"Something's wrong!"

"Mom, please! It's okay," I whispered.

Then Mom said very loudly, for all to hear, "I'll be right downstairs in the rec room. I'll be back in a little while, Lisa." As she went toward the stairs, she took one last look back at Adam, then stared at me. She caught my eye and shook her head slightly in a *no*. It was the same little movement she made when she didn't think the dress I was trying on in a store was right for me. Well, Adam wasn't a dress! I liked everything about Adam; he was real! And I hated all those stupid paperweights because they were so fake, and I hated the *Oh, have you gotten some new ones?* from her fake friends when they visited. And Adam didn't have any idea what was happening, and I liked him for that, too. To him the paperweights were probably just shiny colored things with shells and flowers

69

embedded inside like magic. And Mom was a crumb, I thought, not finding out until later that she was downstairs crying her eyes out because—I don't know why—because of me, or Adam, or me *and* Adam, or because I had failed her, or she had failed me, or all of those, or none.

2

ADAM LIKED MY photos. Not all of them; he wasn't that turned on by my study of Lake Hills' stores, which was good. I hate the phony praise that people give just to be agreeable. Kim does that sometimes. So does Kim's mother. They're so polite.

Mom isn't; she tells me what she thinks of my pictures every time. As well as my clothing and friends. How, *how* can Mom spend weeks, months, doing volunteer work at a county daycare center for low-income people and then be upset about Adam? Yet I knew she would be. She can collect paperweights, really expensive ones from all over the world, then suddenly give a whole bunch of them to be auctioned for charity. She's nuts. So is the world. So am I.

Anyway, Adam liked my pictures. And the darkroom. I was going to give him a short course on how you develop film, but he knew all about it from some books he'd read. He understood what all the tanks and trays were for, and even knew how the enlarger worked. All from books in the library. It was becoming obvious that his real home away from home wasn't that outhouse, but the library.

Adam liked my room, too. I'd cleaned it up quite a bit the night before. But it was still within the broad category of messy, which I think helped relax him, which in turn helped relax me. I was on such a high with Adam and my photos and all, that I'd almost forgotten about Mom's stellar performance. My bed was covered with glossy prints. Adam was looking at my spider series while munching on popcorn with melted cheese, my own special gloppy creation. And there I was, imitating Mom again, getting antsy about melted cheese on my glossies. You can't win; it's all in the genes, right? Just then the phone rang, cutting into our intimate picture-viewing session. It was Kim.

"How's it going, lover lips?" she asked, with a put-on sexy voice.

"Kim, not now!"

"Has your mother gone bananas about you-know-who?"

"Probably. I'm not sure. I'll call you later."

"Don't do anything I wouldn't do," said Miss Brilliant.

"There's *nothing* you wouldn't do. Good-bye, Kim."

"I hope I got you nice and nervous. Toodles, Lee Lee."

"Go skip rope in some quicksand, Kimberly." That's her real name, which I only use in moments of peak exasperation.

Adam had stopped looking at my photos during the high-level phone conference. He was studying my stereo equipment now: turntable, tape deck, receiver, the works. Mom and Dad had indulged me on my thirteenth birthday. To be honest, they indulge me too much, probably because I'm their one and only adorable child. But I'm not spoiled. Much.

"I thought you had a stereo s-system downstairs," said Adam.

"We do," I said. "That's the family's, or I should say, my parents'. This one's mine. Do you want me to put something on?"

"Maybe later . . . I don't know much about m-music. Do you have Michael Jackson?"

73

"Sure. We could watch him on TV. I've got a video cassette. Actually, it's Kim's on loan."

"You've got a video player, too?"

"My parents have." Thinking about his house, I was beginning to feel awful.

"We've got a TV, that's all. You're lucky to be so rich. Even your bathroom is like a m-museum with all that glass stuff on the shelves there. You're lucky. . . ."

He'd gone to the john before and now I realized how it must have looked to him, with more of Mom's shells and paperweights, the sunken bathtub, the soaps on ropes, and so on, compared to his smelly wooden outhouse. Oh, brother.

I didn't know what to say. How do you answer someone who says you're rich, particularly when you *are* pretty rich? My Dad earned every penny of it, but he's doing okay, I guess. I felt guilty and ashamed, sitting there in my luxurious bedroom with built-in bookcases and my stack of stereo components, and my cameras all over my desk.

"When I get out of college," I said, "I don't want all this junk. I don't want to be tied down to junk. Except for the cameras; they're necessities. And I want to travel all over, maybe work for a newspaper or magazine, and take photos."

"Like a reporter?"

"Photojournalist, they call it. Look at this." I pulled

down a book from the top shelf. It had photographs taken during the 1930's Depression when people were out of work, and we had this huge drought in the south-central United States. The soil turned to dust and created dust storms—the dust bowl, they called it—and everybody was suffering. "Look at this picture of a mother and her two hungry kids," I said. "It's by Dorothea Lange, my superhero."

"It's good," said Adam. "That mother looks all s-sad and angry at the same time."

Yes! He saw it! He saw it! Why was that so important to me? Well, it was. He turned the page. There was the Walker Evans picture that always got me close to tears. That scrawny family in their rickety shack, the girl standing by the iron bed. So beaten down, all of them. So frail looking, so beautiful. I wondered what Adam would see in this one. Why was I testing him like this? Maybe I needed solid proof that he was going to be worth bucking Mom, Dad, friends, and flag for.

"What do you think of it?" I asked.

"I think the girl is like my s-sister. And that woman's like my m-mother. You feel sorry for them, but then you look and you look and you can see that they're stronger than you."

"Stronger? Those people are weak. You could blow them away."

"No. Look at their eyes. See? It's like they're saying, 'Th-this is my house. These are my people. So you just go to hell; we're okay.' "

Could he be right? I'd never seen *that* in it. Is that what Walker Evans had wanted to capture? But it didn't really matter. A great work of art—and this was art—can have a lot of meanings. Most likely, Adam was thinking about himself and his own house and family. Well, that's what great photography should do: make you jump into the picture and live in it yourself.

"I see what you're saying, Adam."

"I'll bet they survived," he said. "Like my mother . . ."

Well, I'll tell you this: if Adam isn't one of the brightest kids I've ever met, then I'm Miss Piggy. Whoops, I shouldn't say that; sometimes I *am* Miss Piggy. Check *moi* out in any Chinese restaurant.

Adam had passed whatever dumb test I'd created and then some. The moment was ripe; my question about photographing his house and his family for that photo contest was burning me up. The thought flashed, as it would again, that I was just using him. No! I liked him. I really liked him. But it was the perfect subject for me, for what I felt and thought.

"Adam, uh—this is going to be a little weird," I said. "I'm into photography in a big way, as you can see, right? And there's this photo contest at the library.

And I'd very much like to, well, to photograph your house, the inside and outside, and you and your family. Would it be okay?"

"They're n-not my family. And it isn't my house. So if it's okay with them, it's okay with me. But why *us*?"

"Well, as I was saying, they have awards for different categories, including photo essay, and your house is, like, early American and unusual. So I'd like to enter some photos if they came out good—not as terrific as Dorothea Lange's, that's impossible for me—but good. Would that be all right?"

"I don't want anybody to make fun of them, my m-mother or Emily. They have to look okay."

"Oh, these would be serious pictures! I want to show how great your family is. It would be pictures, say, of Emily playing or your mother cooking. Things like that. Is that all right?"

"Well . . . I guess so. If you give Ma and Emily c-copies for them to have. They like pictures."

"I'd love to give them copies. You, too." It was going to be great! I was already framing shots in my mind. Emily climbing in and out of those tires. Adam swinging her. His mother making muffins in that old oven. Thinking of those muffins I was suddenly hungry.

"Would you like some more of my melted-cheese popcorn?" I asked Adam, as I scooped up a handful.

77

"No thanks. But it's good popcorn. Did you ever make fried apples?"

"No. I never heard of that."

"I invented my own way. I fry them with butter and maple syrup."

"That sounds great!"

"Yeah. You know, we could—no, I guess not. . . ."

"What?"

"Remember that place I showed you in the woods where I take stuff up to eat and I sit there and l-listen? We . . . well, we could bring stuff there and have, like, a picnic."

"I guess we could." I heard my own voice, and it wasn't wildly enthusiastic. I wanted to go. But that Vega-X business was still sort of spooky, no matter how I tried to forget about it. Maybe a picnic alone in the woods wasn't the best idea in the world. Not yet. Could I get Kim and Russ to join us?

"I could bring fried apples. And chicken. Do you want to? W-would you?" He was close to pleading again.

"Sure," I said. "But I've got an idea. You know that picnic area at Green Lake? The one right next to the beach?"

"No. I don't go there. I only swim in my pond."

"It's too cold to swim at Green Lake yet, at least for me—though some of the kids swim there by now,

78

and I guess for you it would seem warm. Anyway, why not have a picnic *there*? Okay? And maybe I'll invite Kim—you met her in the library, remember—and maybe Russ. She hangs out with Russ. And they could bring some stuff, too. Kim makes a great potato salad. What do you think?'' What would *Kim* think, I wondered. Well, I'd worry about that later.

"Okay . . . When?"

"This Saturday?"

"Okay. I'll make enough fried apples and chicken for four."

"Terrific. But let me bring the chicken."

This had been the most normal conversation I'd had with him yet. Not a word about you-know-what. But he was looking kind of tense.

"Do they g-go out together a lot?" he asked. "Kim and R-Russ?"

"All the time. Why do you ask?" I was worried that I may have done the opposite of what I'd meant to do, that is, keep it low-keyed. Because Kim and Russ hang out together, it meant to him that *we* were—Oh, brother!

"Well, I n-never . . . I n-never went out with a girl. And I don't know how to—I mean . . ." He was reddening beautifully. And was he uptight! "I-I never even ever k-kissed a girl."

What boy in the world would ever have admitted that but him? You will have to believe that to me, at this moment, Adam was cute, lovable, and one big teddy bear all at the same time. I kicked the door to my room shut with my foot. Lisa, the nut, was on the loose.

"Oh," I said. "And you're sort of uptight about it, right?" I was plenty uptight by now, too, but I tried not to show it.

"R-right," he said.

"Okay, nuts to that! *I've* never really actually kissed a boy. Are you ready? Then let's plunge in and get it over with right now!" I sat next to him on the bed, wrecking two of my glossy prints under my big rear end, and guided his arms around me. I wrapped mine around him in the clumsiest embrace in the history of New Jersey. Suddenly we both burst out laughing. I moved my face to within an inch of his face and we burst out laughing again. Then we kissed slightly, then again slightly more, then once more—a very good long solid kiss. The next one was all Adam's; he did it beautifully.

I moved away a little to give us a chance to breathe. We weren't laughing anymore.

"Now we don't have to be nervous."

"Yeah. That was nice."

"If you say they do it better on Vega-X I'll punch you right in the face."

80

Adam laughed and so did I. Of everything that happened that day, his laughter just then was the best thing of all. It's hard to put into words, but his laughing was healthy. Because he was laughing at himself, I thought. At the whole planet Vega-X thing. He knew it was all bull. I hoped.

But all good moments must come to an end. Mom was knocking at the bedroom door. Perfect timing.

"Lisa! Are you there?"

"Yes, Mother!" I was *not* happy. This was the limit!

"Please open the door!"

"It's open, Mother!"

"It's unlocked, but not open. Please open it!"

I leaned over and opened the door. There was Mom, her eyes red from crying, her hair messed, standing with her hands on her hips as if she were about to play Simon Says. "Please have your door open when you have guests!" How totally, utterly embarrassing. Nice work, Mom.

"Can we talk about it later?" I asked.

"You can talk about it all you want. But please leave that door open when you have guests." She never said anything like that when Kim was over. But of course she didn't mean *guest*; she meant *boy*. Great! Between Adam's mother with her "Adam's got a girlfriend," and my mother's "leave the door open," it was a dead tie for the world's gross parent championship. Never in my life had I wanted to be twenty-two and on my own as much as at that moment. I'd have settled for eighteen. Seventeen, even.

My mother turned and walked a few steps toward the stairs, stopped, then turned back. "You really ought to sew up your pants, Adam," she said.

That did it! I blew my fuse! And in the worst possible way. "Mother, I think you're smashed!"

"How dare you!" There were instant tears. She turned and hurried toward the stairs.

I rose and walked to the door, then stopped. One part of me wanted to run after her and tell her I was sorry, I hadn't meant it. But another part of me was saying how *dare* she insult my friend.

Adam was next to me by now. I guess I was crying a little, too. "I feel so—so ashamed," I blurted. "I—I—I'm sorry, Adam."

"My father hollered at us all the time," said Adam. "And he used a-a belt on me. So don't worry about me. And don't cry. You didn't do anything."

I tried to take some deep breaths. "Thanks. Thanks, Adam." A belt? Good grief! Maybe it wasn't all so warm and cozy at the Bates home after all.

"I better go, right?" he asked.

"I—I guess so. It's pretty messy around here right now. I'll get you your bike."

"Hey, Lisa, I'm s-sorry. Don't worry about Sat-

82

urday. Or your mother. I'm going to sew up my jeans for you.''

As if that would solve everything. I laughed; I couldn't help it, even though I was still half crying, too. That's what Laurel and Hardy would have said. Or Steve Martin.

"I guess it's a good idea," I said. "To sew them up."

"I think they'll let me . . . See, I'm supposed to let p-people laugh at me. That's what they want."

"Adam, that doesn't make sense. Believe me, it doesn't."

"Yes, it does! It's to test me. To make me s-strong. Like those people in that picture you showed me."

Back to square one. Why did that stupid idea have to keep pressing down on his skull like an iron hat? Why couldn't he be normal? He looked perfectly normal as I walked him to the corner, his bike between us. He looked perfectly normal riding north toward the hills where he lived. I watched until he disappeared around a turn in the road. He *looked* perfectly normal. But somewhere in all the delicate things that make up a brain, and a person, and a personality, there was this streak or scar, like on a photo negative. And you can't get it out, no matter how you try. Every time you make a print, it's still there. And the way the world is, it always happens to the pictures you love the most.

83

8

EVERYTHING WAS A total mess. I didn't know what to do first. I had to clean up the popcorn and photos all over my bed, and do some studying—we were having a test on the circulatory system in science on Friday—and worry about asking Kim to go on that picnic, and cope with Mom's depressed anger, and think about the photo series, and this and that and the other. I decided to start by cleaning up the stray popcorn. I ate it.

While I tried to get myself organized I could hear Mom in the kitchen below, preparing dinner—it wasn't my cooking day, thank goodness—and the sharp sounds of pans and bowls had an angry edge that I'd learned to "read" from early childhood. If I'd gone down to apologize—not that I felt like it—I'd have been met with a barrage of flak.

The phone rang while I was filling out my entry form for the contest. I answered on the upstairs extension while Mom picked up in the kitchen; we have extensions everywhere but on the roof. Mom said, "Hello." I said, "Hello." Mom said, "Oh!" I said, "Oh, oh." Not the best reaction. It was Kim again. Mom hung up abruptly, without her normal *Oh, hello, Kim. How are you? Here's Lisa. Bye-bye.*

Kim can read the signs, too. "What's wrong?" she asked. "Has the you-know-what hit the fan?"

"Oh, has it!" I said.

"Is Adam still there?"

"No."

"Need some moral support? I can come over right now if you want."

Good old Kim, always there, true and blue, when needed. "I'm okay," I said. "I think. I hope. I don't really know yet."

"Want to talk?"

Oh, did I! I wanted to talk about picnics, and about real friendships, and real people, and about Kim please-don't-let-me-down. "Kim, listen. Don't say a word. Just listen. Please. Adam wanted to go on a picnic sort of thing, alone with me near his house, out in the woods, and I thought it was too much. Are you listening?"

"I'm right here."

"So I suggested—oh, brother—that, well, maybe we could all have a picnic this Saturday at Green Lake, meaning you and Russ, too. And I know what you said, Kim, the other day. But Adam really is a good guy, Kim, and I like him and I . . . I need this, Kim."

"You got it. Okay?"

"Kim? Thank you. I mean it. Thank you."

"No problem."

"But what about Russ?"

"Oh, him. The Hulk. I can deliver the body, but I can't promise I can deliver the mind. He thinks Adam's a real weirdo, Lee. He says in gym, in the locker room, even in the shower, Adam won't take off his T-shirt. Stuff like that. I'm warning you."

"You talked about Adam to Russ?"

"Come on, Lisa. I knew you'd want to go out. I was trying to, well, ease the way. Russ isn't really all wrong, Lee; you *know* that. Anyway, I couldn't make a dent."

"Will he—will he make fun of Adam, or start something?"

"Of course not! I mean, what do you think Russ is? He has a very gentle side, Lee, only he doesn't show it. In public, that is. He'll be okay. Believe me. Have faith."

"Thanks, Kim."

And then, *wham*, the phone clicked and my mother was on again. Good grief, had she been listening all this time? No, Mom would never do that. Impossible. Or was it? Times they were a-changing, with her little darling clearly in the clutches of an evil maniac who had torn jeans. But no, no, I'd heard that receiver go down, loud and clear, before.

"Lisa," Mom said, "would you *mind* keeping this short! I'm expecting a call, and it's important. You're always on that *phone!*"

"Yes, Mother," I said, trying to sound meek.

"I'm *sorry*, Kim!" BANG! She'd hung up abruptly again. Way to go, Mom!

"Okay, Kim. You heard," I said.

"I can't believe that was your mother."

"That *wasn't* my mother. That was . . . someone else. If you know what I mean."

"Not exactly . . . but . . . Hey, listen. Call me later, if you want, or come on over. Okay?"

"Okay. Thanks again, Kim. Thanks."

"Oh! Lee? What should I plan to bring? I mean picnic-wise?"

"Potato salad. And Russ. Mayonnaise on both."

"Okay. How about bathing suits? The lake's warming up."

"Is it? Okay. Wait till you see Adam swim. He's unbelievable!"

"Nude?"

"Come on, Kimberly! Hey, I'd better get off before my mother blows all her fuses."

"So long, Lee Lee."

"So long."

I skimmed through my science text, trying not to think about Adam, Mom, or the real universe. But I could sense the anger from the kitchen floating up the stairs, against gravity, along with the odor of scorched broccoli. Mom scorches things only when she's sore. It was going to be quite a dinner.

Dad got home at six-thirty, and I slowly migrated downstairs. We gathered in the dining alcove, as usual. Only Mom wasn't speaking to anyone. She set out three cups of fresh fruit salad and in the huge silence the little clicks of the cups sounded like cannon shots. And each sharp click said, *See, Lisa, you ungrateful, rebellious daughter with your horrible taste in boys and your vicious tongue, see what you've done to your loving, all-suffering, wonderful, dear poor mother!* All that in those tiny clicks.

The silence filled the room like a gigantic feather

pillow that had burst open. When would Dad come to the rescue? He seemed to be acting as if the cold shoulder was being aimed at him. Maybe this was the continuation of something going on between *them*. Maybe I was getting tangled in their web somehow.

Okay! I resolved to be the only adult at that table and end the cold war. But how? I would find something so mature to say that their mouths would drop in amazed admiration. I downed some more cantaloupe and orange chunks, deep in thought.

"Uh—Dad? Mom and I have just had a slight difference of opinion that, uh, has escalated. I'm sorry for the escalation, Mom." Very United Nations, right?

Click went her spoon. Another cannon shot.

"What difference of opinion?" asked Dad.

"Oh. Well this boy in one of my classes came over to see my photos, because I want to take some shots of his house, and, uh, well he's different and—"

"Different!" Mom said, throwing the word out like a dagger. "He looks like one of those dropouts that hang around outside the shopping mall. Like a mall rat! He looks bizarre! I don't understand you, Lisa! As for escalation, you virtually called me a drunk in front of that—that *person*!"

"Mother, you started it. You know what you said to him was rude!"

"And what was it that *you* said!" Mom countered.

89

"Hey, hey, hold on," said Dad, caught in the cross-fire. "You said, she said— Come on, this could go on all night. Let's hear Lisa's side, Phyllis. Okay? Let's give her a break. It's not as if she's brought home a stash of drugs or something."

"That'll be next!"

"Mom, chill out, please!" So much for the U.N.

"Don't you use that mouth of yours on me! Don't start telling me what—"

"Okay! Okay! Okay! . . . Dad. Mom. Listen. Please! I am not marrying him! I admit he may look a little strange—"

"A *little*—"

"Mom, please. But he's very nice and he's bright —he spends half his time in the library—and he's had, I guess, a tough life. And I may as well tell you right now that he lives up in the hills—yes, *those* hills, Mom—but I met his mother and she's very warm and generous, and his little sister, and she's so sweet and nice and—"

"You seem to have met his entire clan!"

"Everybody makes fun of him! And I like him! And I want to take pictures of him and his family and his house for that photo contest at the library. And I'm going on a picnic with him and Russ and Kim on Saturday, and I'm telling you now, and I mean it,

90

there's no way you're going to stop me, so we may as well be adult about it! He's my friend, and I'm his friend, and I'd be ashamed of you, Mom and Dad, I really would, if you wouldn't let me go out with a boy just because his pants are ripped, or he's poor, or he happens to have a stammer.''

"Is this the way it's going to be, Lisa?" said Mom. "The first boy you've ever gone out with, and you're laying down the law to us. Is that it? Fourteen, and you think you can tell us where to get off?"

"No! If I said I was going to stay out till two in the morning, that's different. But this is a daytime picnic and—"

"Sweets, I think—"

"Dad. Please. No 'Sweets.' "

"Okay. Whatever your name is—Hey you!—I think you've made a good case. By the way, speaking of names, what's the boy's name we're talking about?"

"Adam Bates."

"And you like Adam?"

"Yes."

"And you think he's okay, correct?"

"Yes."

Dad looked at Mom and shrugged. "How can we not let her use her own head?"

"Herb, you haven't met the boy."

91

"I know. But I think I've met Lisa. Once or twice in passing. Right, Swee— Right, Lisa?"

"Yes. Thank you, Dad."

Mom did not look too good, I'm afraid. Her face had darkened. "I think we might have discussed this in private first, Herb," she said. "I think my opinion is due that much respect."

"You're right," Dad answered. "But I've said what I've said. I think we have to let Lisa start using the fourteen years we've given her. I trust her. Period."

"And you trust this hillbilly, too?" Mom said.

"He's not a hillbilly, Mom! I'm really surprised at you! I really am!"

"I trust Lisa's judgment, Phyllis. You can be damn sure I'm just as concerned as you are."

"Oh, *are* you!"

"Mom, Dad, *please*! Cool it, *please*! Adam is okay. He's not some sort of sex maniac. He's never even kissed a girl in his whole life. It's actually none of your business, but I'm telling you so you can see. Okay?"

"How do you know he's never kissed a girl?" asked Mom.

"Because he said so."

"And you believe him?"

"Yes!"

"Why would he start telling you things like that?"

"Mom, you're giving me the third degree! Leave me alone!"

"No, I won't leave you alone! You're telling us everything is just wonderful. Yet you've just barely met him and he's talking about kissing."

"Oh for crying out tears, Mom, you don't know what kids talk about! He's so naive. He's so, so— Mom, he was afraid to touch my hand. Okay? Okay? Do you want me to draw pictures? You can't believe what some kids are doing! And he's afraid to touch my hand!" I was at the point of tears. Was this what my next four years were going to be like?

"All right, Lisa," said Mom, her voice softening for the first time. "I believe you. I just wish it had been someone else."

"It's just a *picnic*, Mom."

"I know. I know." She did not seem reassured.

"I'm sorry for what I said, Mom—in my room before. Okay? I really am. I've been meaning, you know, to say that all evening."

"Thank you. I'm sorry for what I said, too," she answered.

"I now pronounce you mother and daughter," said Dad. "Now can we finish our fruit salad?"

Peace descended, at least for the moment. But I felt

I was sitting on a sort of lie all through dinner. Because forthright though they thought I was, I hadn't said one single solitary word about Vega-X. And if they trusted me—which Dad had made into a big thing—and if I wasn't telling them about that, wasn't I being a class-A fraud? The answer kept rubbing up against me like an itchy cat. The answer was yes.

9

GREEN LAKE WAS absolutely glorious that Saturday. The beach was loaded with kids, and some adults, too. A perfect blue-sky day, with a whiff of summer in the air, though it was still a week till Memorial Day. There was a bunch of little kids in the water even though the docks and ropes hadn't been set up yet. They didn't look cold; in fact, they were having a ball. It's funny, the younger kids were all in, swimming, but only a few teenagers would swim, and no adults. It happens that way every spring; the little kids are always ahead of the rest. In spite of all the talk about bathing suits, we four wore jeans. Adam had sewn his up with bright red thread, which looked so outrageous it was great.

We had flopped down where the grass and trees meet the sandy part of the beach, sand brought in and dumped from somewhere else, of course. Our blankets were spread—my famous red and orange one, and Kim's blue-lagoon special—and there we were, stretched out, with my head on Adam's stomach, and Russ's head on the bags of food. Russ thought he was being funny. The only other pillow he would accept was Kim's rear end, but she constantly twisted away from him. I think Adam was slightly shocked. He'd even seemed uncomfortable when I'd put my head on his stomach.

Russ had said hello to Adam with a real upbeat, and had even said "Hey, that's a real good old bike," when he'd seen Adam's super clunker. No put-downs at all. Kim's doing, I assumed. But I had to give Russ credit; he was being aces, as they say in the old-time movies. Even when one of his buddies came over and they did their grunt routine—*Hiya. Hiya. Yeah, what's happenin'? I dunno, what's goin' on? Yeah, I dunno*—Russ actually introduced Adam to his friend Frank.

"Hey, uh, this is, uh, Adam. Hey, Adam, meet Frank."

"Yeah, hi," came from Frank. "What's happenin'?"

"H-h-hi."

"Yeah. See you aroun'." Frank took a pull on his cigarette and rejoined his group with the blasting mega-radio down the beach.

But Russ, being Russ, made a quick grab for Kim's posterior. "Come on, Kim. My head's gettin' sore. Move your rear end over."

"No! Cut it out!"

"Why? What's so precious about your rear?"

"Russell! We are at a public beach! I happen to know those people over there. They're friends of my mother."

"Oh, yeah? So what? I need a pillow. Hey, Adam, would you loan me Lisa? I'll pay rent."

I felt a rush of defensiveness for Adam. I didn't think he could deal with this wise-mouth stuff. He didn't seem to realize that Russ was just putting us on. I tried to keep cool as I lay there; I pressed my head hard against Adam's stomach, as if nailing myself to him.

"Uh . . . I d-don't think you should," Adam said to Russ.

"Oh, my! He d-doesn't think I should," Russ mimicked him.

So much for Russ the ace. What did Kim *see* in him? That had to be the pits, imitating someone's stammer. I was getting nicely steamed up. The only reason I kept my mouth shut was that, though I could feel him tense up, Adam just lay there. Maybe he hadn't really noticed. I wasn't sure, so why mess up the whole afternoon.

But Kim didn't let it go by. "Russ, I can't believe you," she said.

"What'sa matter? What'd I do?"

"I'm just warning you, Russ. Don't do that again," she said.

"Yeah, yeah, yeah."

"Russ! I mean it!"

"Okay! Lay off, will you! Man, you'd think I robbed a bank! It's all because you're so uptight about letting me rest my head on your—"

Something exploded suddenly. Adam was up from under me, and my head bounced on the ground. For a horrendous second I thought he was going to punch Russ. But he was running toward the lake. And could he run! He just kept going on into the water, taking wide leaping steps, then a long dive. I didn't know what was going on. Was he angry, and was this some sort of release, like hitting a punching bag? Or was he suddenly showing off? I couldn't tell. He was gone. Under the water, up again, then down.

We were all standing now. Then I saw it. A hand.

Just a hand opening and closing and thrashing the water quite a distance out. There was this huge burst of water and up came Adam like a whale surfacing, and there was this kid in his right arm. By now three or four other guys were in the water, all swimming toward Adam. But Adam was already swimming back, his right arm under the boy's shoulder, churning the water with his left in the most amazing, crazy rescue stroke ever seen.

Adam laid the kid down on the beach and turned his head sideways and started pumping his chest, and the water just poured out.

"I'm a lifeguard! I'm a lifeguard!" a tall teenager called out. "You're doing it wrong! Let me do it!"

"Where the hell *were* you, if you're supposed to be a lifeguard?" someone shouted.

"Not on duty till Memorial Day," the teenager said as he took over from Adam.

The weird ending to this was that the kid was okay, but his mother came down from way back in the wooded area, where she'd probably been totally oblivious, and gave the boy a tremendous smack on his rear end. The kid started howling. Not a word of thanks to Adam; not the slightest sign of knowing that her kid had almost drowned.

"Lady, your son was drowning!" I called to her.

"I told him not to go out so deep!"

"He just saved your son's life!" I said, pointing toward Adam, who was on his way back to our blanket.

"Well, what does he want? A reward?" She gave us a look as if we were a bunch of hoods, then dragged her kid, still howling, back with her to the wooded area.

But that downer was balanced out by Russ's doing something aces again. He went over and shook Adam's hand and said in his best macho mumble, "Man, that was A-okay. Yeah. Yeah. You were great."

"Uh . . . huh?" said Adam, my Adam, superhero of the day. He hardly knew he'd done anything. A slight smile flickered, then disappeared. It seemed as if he couldn't, or wouldn't, take praise.

Kim and Russ strolled down the beach toward the blasting radio, while Adam and I plopped down on our blanket again.

"How did you ever *see* that kid?" I asked.

"I was watching them swimming," said Adam. "That's because I always watch Emily."

"Wow," I said, "you're soaked to the skin, just like the other day. You're always all wet, you know?"

"I know. . . ."

"Come on, take off your shirt," I said.

"No. I'm okay."

"Come on. The sun's great. I wish I had my bathing suit."

I started to tug at his T-shirt in playful Lisa Daniels style as he lay there on his stomach, but as I pulled it up, he screamed, "No! Don't!" In that brief moment, I'd seen his back.

"I said no! I said no!"

His back was a crisscrossed red-and-brown surface of raised scars. It had to have come from being beaten. Beaten over and over again, all over his back. Oh, Adam . . . I didn't know what to say. I didn't know what to do.

"I'm sorry. I'm sorry, Adam."

He was up and walking back toward the woods, toward his bike among the trees.

"Adam, please. Wait!"

"I t-told you not to," he said as he walked. "I said no!"

I ran after him and caught up, but then he started running. I ran as fast as I could, but he was on his bike.

"Adam, please! Listen to me for a minute!"

"I told you not to!" He started pedaling, but I lunged forward and pulled him off the bike. We were both on the ground, half twined together, with the bike over our legs.

"Adam, I don't care! I don't care! You don't have to be ashamed or—or bothered about *anything* with me. Please, Adam! Look at me!"

"What!" He looked straight at me as he pushed the bike aside.

"You asked me to go with you and see that capsule. And I did, right? Okay! Now go along with *me*."

"W-what do you mean?"

"Don't move! Don't say anything! And don't move!" I wasn't quite sure what I would do; I was going on pure instinct.

First I kissed him on his cheek, then on his lips, then, lying there on the ground, I pulled up his T-shirt and rubbed him on his back all over, above his waist, along his spine, at his shoulders, everywhere. He shuddered a little and tensed. But then he started to relax; I could feel it. Incredible. I'd managed to do something right. I relaxed, too, and kissed his back very gently. Finally, I kissed him on the lips again. We lay there not saying a word.

"So what do you think?" I finally asked.

"I think . . . I w-won't go home."

"Good."

"I think . . . I l-like you a lot, Lisa."

"I like you a lot, too. I really do, Adam."

"Thank you."

"Oh, brother . . . You don't have to thank me for liking you. Anyway, do you want to talk about, you know, *this*?" I touched his back gently.

"No. He's g-gone now, my father. . . . Sometimes I still have bad dreams. . . . That's all. . . . He beat my mother, too. . . ."

"And Emily?"

"No. She was too young, I g-guess. Don't tell them!" he said, gesturing toward Kim and Russ down on the beach, strolling back toward our blankets. "They'll just laugh at me."

"Oh, no they won't! Nobody would!"

"Kids used to, back in el-elementary school."

"Well, Russ and Kim wouldn't! Only a birdbrain would!"

"Russ made f-fun of me, before."

"Oh . . . Well, I know— But not about *this*!"

"But I think he thinks I'm okay now b-because I helped that kid."

"Well, I think you're okay no matter what you do. A-okay! But enough serious stuff. Let's beat them to some of that chicken before Russ eats it all. Which he would, the birdbrain!"

10

MRS. FELTS WALKED up and down the room, handing back our graded test papers on the circulatory system. From the test scores anyone could see that we now knew almost as much about the heart, arteries, veins, and blood cells—including hemoglobin—as any intelligent chimpanzee. It was bad. Every so often you could hear a distinct groan from some new lucky winner. I was expecting the worst; I'd hardly cracked my book last week. Great way to start us off on a Monday morning, Mrs. Smile-Awhile! But when I finally got my own paper back, to my disbelief, I'd pulled a ninety-six. And there was a note in red: *Nice work, Lisa!* I jammed the paper into my backpack, fast. She might as well have written: *Nice work, Miss Class Nerd.*

What was even more of a surprise was Adam's grade; he'd gotten a pair of eights. Eighty-eight, and he never paid any attention in class. How did he do it?

While our zoo keeper was still busily handing out the tests, I leaned over and whispered to Adam, "Hey. You studied about hemoglobin after all."

"No, I didn't," he answered. "I just g-guessed everything."

"Bull."

"Well . . . I read the b-book for about ten minutes."

"Double bull. What are you doing after school today?"

"I don't know. I'm going to get a job at the Lake Hills Mall."

"A job? What job?"

"There's a job open. They need somebody at Paul's Pizza Place. W-what are you doing after?"

"Well, I've got to buy film and enlarging paper and stuff for, you know, the photo series. I could get it at the mall. We could meet there."

"Okay. Like a date?"

"Sort of," I said. "Date" sounded so formal. I wanted to say we could just hang out there awhile, but Mrs. Felts was back at her desk, and I didn't want to have another Smile-Awhile incident, so I called, "Shh! Later!" to Adam and faced front.

"I see," said Mrs. Felts, "that—ahem—*blood* has flowed on our circulatory system test." Oh, brother! The Smiler had made a funny. No one laughed. Dead silence in the room. "Maybe you just didn't have the *heart* for it." Good grief! She was becoming a stand-up comedian. "I'm afraid it was a *vain* endeavor for most of you."

The class moaned. And for the second time in this century, Mrs. Adrienne Felts smiled. What a sadist! I think she needs a shrink. Or a better gag writer.

Adam and I met at the main entrance to the Lake Hills Mall at three-thirty. Adam was sitting outside on a low cement wall along the strip of scrubby bushes and plants that's supposed to make the entrance area look beautiful. Some chance. That wall was famous; kids sat there in good weather, waiting for their parents to pick them up, or waiting for friends, or just hanging out, usually with a box blasting out some hard rock or punk.

As I got closer, I could see that Adam didn't look too happy. He was sitting alone, as always, far from everybody else. I nodded hello to some kids I knew, then hitched myself up onto the wall next to Adam. He was frowning.

"Glad to see you, too!" I said.

"H-hi."

"Hi. What's wrong?"

"I went to Paul's Pizza. They s-said I have to be over sixteen."

"I should have known."

"They l-laughed at me while I was walking out."

"So we'll never buy any pizzas there again." He still looked very down. "Come on, Adam. You can't be, you know, so sensitive. Cheer up! *I'm* here. We're supposed to be sort of on a date. Remember?"

"Y-yeah." Still pretty somber. So I pushed closer to him on the wall, very close, and gave him a little kiss on the cheek. Followed by three more, rapid fire.

Adam shrugged, the way he does when he's embarrassed, and hitched slightly away. I hitched toward him and gave him another quick kiss. He hitched away again.

"Everybody can s-see us here," he said, nodding toward the crowd of kids along the wall.

"Don't worry about it; they're not watching us," I said. "They do the same thing. You really care about what people think, don't you? It's funny; I thought you didn't."

"No. I don't care."

"Yes, you do."

"I don't!'

"But you looked so unhappy, just because some-

107

body laughed at you in the pizza place.''

"No. It's that I need a job. I d-don't have any money for anything. I can't go out with you because I don't have any m-money.''

"Who needs money? We could take a walk. Or ride our bikes out to the lake. Besides, I've got some do-re-mi.''

"No!''

"Oh, come on, Adam. That's primeval, you having to pay. No way. If you have some cash and I don't, then you can pay for things; if I have it, I'll pay; if we're both loaded at the time, we'll both pay. Doesn't that make sense?''

"Yeah . . . But on Vega-X nobody has to pay for anything.'' Oh, no! Vega-X again!

"Okay. Fine. When we date on Vega-X, we'll just pull the burgers and shakes off the trees like apples.''

"Don't m-make fun of me!''

"I'm not making fun of you. It's just . . . Adam, can't you quit with this Vega-X stuff? You know it's all bull.''

"No! No! It's true!'' He slid off the wall and walked about five steps away, then turned toward me defiantly. "It's true!''

I'd done it! I'd promised myself to pay no attention to his Vega-X fantasies. To be cool about it, like his

108

mother. Instead, I'd called him a liar.

I slid down off the wall and went over to him. "Okay. Okay. I'm sorry." I took his hand and squeezed hard. "I'm sorry, Adam. Peace?"

"Don't make fun of me about Vega-X, Lisa. D-don't."

"I won't. I didn't mean to . . . Come on, I've got to buy film and junk. Let's head in."

We strolled around in the mall, hand in hand, which changed after a while to arms around each other's waists. I'd envied kids walking like that for a long time; now all this was mine, as they say in those old romantic ballads. But I wasn't totally at peace because of the jagged edge of that Vega-X business. I felt it like a pebble in my shoe. Every time I thought Adam was perfectly okay, every time I began to feel really at ease and comfortable with him he dropped another Vega-X firecracker, and I was back on standby alert. I liked walking arm in arm, and it was fun going in and out of stores looking at priced-down clothes, and gag gifts, and books, and posters, and records, and what not. But still, the pebble was there in my shoe, and because of it, I—*we*—limped slightly in everything we did, if I can stretch an image.

But I'm only human, and nobody wants to carry pebbles around in their shoe all day. So I mentally took

109

the pebble out and tossed it away, and suggested we have some pizza in a place that competes with Paul's. I was starving and couldn't hold out till Mom's fish fiesta at six-thirty.

Over the pizza and sodas, I told Adam the story of my life. I got started because the pizza joint had somehow reminded me of a small restaurant my grandfather had once owned; I'd seen it as a very young kid before Grandpa sold it and retired. I told Adam how my grandfather had come to the United States from Europe as a young man with only the clothes on his back, and how he had worked as a dishwasher, then a waiter, and saved his money and opened a small restaurant in Morristown, New Jersey. The restaurant served mostly cold and hot sandwiches and coffee. And I told Adam how he sent my father to college even though they were poor, and how my father struggled in his early years working on a newspaper, the *Star-Ledger*, then got into the advertising part of newspaper work, and finally got to work in a series of ad agencies in New York. And how my mother had had a pretty similar background, being poor when she was a kid, and how my mother and father met at a mutual friend's party. And hatched me a couple of years later.

I talked on and on, about how I always thought I was ugly—*No, you're not*, Adam said—and always played with paints and crayons. And how I loved to draw but was terrible at it, and very frustrated until I discovered photography, and how I was always pretty much a loner until I met Kim, and always wanted a brother or sister. I rattled on through three slices of pizza with cheese, sausage, *and* anchovies.

Then I asked Adam about his life. To make clear I didn't mean his supposed life on planet Vega-X, I actually used the phrase: "your life up in the hills." I hoped he'd tell me more about his father, and those beatings, and everything.

"Oh . . . I just live there. I d-don't want to talk about it."

"Not at all?" I asked. I guessed it must have been too painful for him. I wondered if he'd ever talked to a psychologist. Didn't they have one at the school? He could certainly use one, with his horrifying childhood, and all those Vega-X fantasies. But I was afraid that if I suggested it he'd think I was calling him a liar again, about Vega. Or that I was saying he was crazy.

"Say something. Anything," I coaxed gently.

"Well, we always have a C-christmas tree because I always cut one down from the top of that hill where we were last week. And . . . I don't know . . . I have to take baths in the kitchen in a big tub, because we don't have a bathtub. We take turns."

111

Maybe that's why he wasn't uptight about swimming without his jeans. "Well, go ahead . . . what else?" I asked, still hoping he'd really start talking freely.

"Well . . . My father used to take me hunting with his f-friends. Once I killed a deer with a rifle. And everyone thought it was g-great. My father, too. The deer kept running, and there was all this blood, and we tracked it by following the blood trail. I guess it finally didn't have any blood left, so it just stopped and sank down and d-died. We watched it dying. I remember my father said, 'The kid got his first deer!' He thought it was g-great. . . ."

"Then what happened?" I asked. There had been some good moments with his father, it seemed, if you can call killing a deer a good moment. At least, it wasn't all beatings.

"I don't know . . . I went home and c-cried, where my father couldn't see me. He hated it when I c-cried. . . ."

"Oh! Well I'm glad you did! I really am. You know, most guys wouldn't admit that they cried about anything."

"So what."

"So I guess it's one of the things I like about you. You don't do what most people do. You're yourself."

"Hey, Lisa! That's funny! Because that's one of the things I l-like about *you*!" He seemed so *up*, suddenly,

112

talking about us, that I decided to lighten the mood and not probe anymore. But I wished he talked more. It was like pulling teeth to get him to say anything about himself.

"We make a matched set," I said. "Bugs Bunny and Daffy Duck. Who else would order pizza with sausage *and* anchovies *and* cheese?"

"I owe you half. Because I'm going to g-get a job and pay you back."

"Okay. Say, Adam . . ."

"What?"

"Do you think . . . I can't believe I'm asking this. Forget it."

"No. Go ahead."

"Do you think I'm okay-looking? I know what you said before, but—"

"I think you're really b-beautiful."

"Oh, come on! Don't exaggerate."

"No, I do! I really do!"

"Well, I know that's bull. But it sounds nice."

"It isn't bull. Everything I say is what I m-mean."

"I know."

"You think *I* look okay?" he asked.

"I think you're kind of sexy."

"What?" He looked embarrassed; his neck turned red.

"You heard me."

113

"Me?"

"Yes, you!"

"Oh, okay. So are you."

"Well, there's only one thing left for us to do *now*!" I am a devil sometimes.

Adam looked pretty nervous. "What's th-that?"

"Go buy my film and enlarging paper."

"Oh."

"You look disappointed. What did you think I was going to say?"

"That you wanted to do some l-laboratory experiments in advanced b-biology." He frowned slightly, trying not to laugh.

"Not me. I have to study the heart a lot more first. Not to mention the brain," I said. "Mrs. Felts would love me."

"Me, too . . . Maybe we'll t-take some advanced biology in high school."

"Or college."

"Or h-high school."

"Or college."

At which point we both cracked up. Planet Vega-X had faded away, and I was getting on a high again. We went completely berserk and ordered another whole pizza. With cheese, sausage, *and* anchovies, naturally.

11

I HAD THE corner of Adam's house in my viewfinder, and a rusty old boiler, and a pile of tires with Emily on top of the pile, playing with her doll. I checked my focus, my shutter, my film speed, then moved slowly sideways while Emily, not noticing me anymore, lifted her doll up to the top of the highest tire as if she had conquered Mount Everest. I shot, wound, shot, wound, as Emily climbed all over the heap of tires, swinging her doll down and around the way Adam had swung *her*.

I moved, camera to my eye, as Emily moved. We

115

moved together like dancers, she leading, me following, in, out, left, right. She kept threatening, she and her doll, to break out of my viewfinder's tight rectangle, but I wouldn't let her; I clung to her, almost knowing where she would move next, almost playing with the doll myself, almost becoming her.

I was so lost in my viewfinder that I'd forgotten Adam was standing right next to me, and I bumped into him as I glided sideways. I didn't move my eye from the camera.

"Sorry, sorry," I said, as I crept slowly left, panning around to get more of the house, to catch Emily against that wonderful kitchen window with the single broken shutter and a torn dish towel hanging out over the sill to dry in the sun.

"Hey, you're like a real p-pro." said Adam, as he did his own slow dance following me.

"Thanks. I've got to concentrate. I'll be done soon."

I'd done the outside and the inside of the house, and had some great shots of Mrs. Bates at the oven, at the sink, and sitting in her old armchair out in the backyard. She had this dilapidated chair back there, for "sunning" as she put it, and it was one of my best shots—her bare arms raised to shade her eyes as she sat among the jungle of wrecked things, like the grand owner of some fabulous sculpture garden.

116

And I had a bunch of shots of Adam swinging Emily around, also great, and shots of him reading on his bed and pumping water at the sink, and so on. For the indoor shots, I'd used another camera loaded with fast film. I came equipped, I can tell you. The pannier I'd attached to my bike was close to bursting with three cameras, a separate flash unit, and a telescoping aluminum tripod—which I didn't use—as well as eight rolls of film.

Even with the map Adam had drawn for me, I'd gotten lost twice as I worked my way up that rutted road—the long route, not the shorter one through the woods—but it was worth it. What a photo series this was going to be! I had close-ups of everything from that old cupboard in the kitchen to the inside of the outhouse, which Emily thought was *yuck!* but Adam thought was funny. I had long views of the fields beyond, and shots of the family together—maybe a little too stiff—and Adam at a window looking out, and you name it. The works. I was in photojournalist paradise.

As I was finishing my shots of Emily, Mrs. Bates called from the door, "Hello, there! Time for apple juice and corn muffins!"

"Oh, great!" I called back. "Are the muffins still in the oven?" I wanted a shot of them while they were still in the pan, with the oven door open.

"They're just about ready to come out, honey!"

"Oh, good! Can I take some pictures of them?"

"Of my muffins? Why of course you can!"

Following my round of authentic early-American baking shots, we took a juice and muffin break. I rattled on about how incredible the photos were going to be, and mentioned that I'd like to split the prize money with them if I won the contest. I hadn't meant any harm by that—it was just me overflowing and bubbling and feeling good about the whole thing. But I'd hit a sensitive spot in Mrs. Bates.

"I know you mean well, honey, but we don't need your prize. That's yours. We folks up here are just fine. We don't need charity."

"But it's not charity! It's pictures of *you*! It's like we're all doing this together," I said.

"Well, Adam said you'd give us some of your pictures. That'd be nice. We'll put them up on the wall."

"But if I win—"

"Honey, we don't need your charity! And we don't need your trailer parks or your welfare, either! We got friends! And we got pride! We go back to the Revolution! I'm sorry, but that's the way it is."

I was really shook. What did I have to do with those officials Adam said wanted to relocate them to a trailer park? Or with the welfare department, for that matter?

118

"I've got nothing to do with things like trailer parks or—"

"Oh, yes, you do, honey! Yes, you do! All you folks down there in Lake Hills. I see your big houses. And your big cars. We don't need your charity. Like I said, we lived here before your grandparents were ever in this country. You and all the folks down in the valley. Seems like we fought the Revolution so that you could come over here and have your big houses and your big cars. Nothing personal, honey."

"It *is* personal!" I said. She was resenting me! This was a new Mrs. Bates! I was the rich, the all-powerful. Just as Mom resented Adam, Mrs. Bates was resenting me, only 180 degrees reversed. What a world!

Adam stepped in, thank goodness. I was ready to jump my sprocket.

"Hey, Ma, you sound just l-like he used to sound. You know *who*."

"Oh . . ." Mrs. Bates seemed to lose some of her steam. "Oh . . . Do I?"

Emily, at the table, wanted to get her two cents in. "Yes, you do," she said.

"You don't even remember him!" said Mrs. Bates.

"Yes, I do," Emily said weakly.

"Well, maybe your father was right in some things!" Mrs. Bates said to Adam. Then she turned back to me.

"The musket balls that Washington's army used, the iron came from the mines in *these* hills. My grandpa worked those same mines. Iron fed us all. Jesse, my husband, worked at Hibernia Forge till they shut it down. Jesse, he couldn't do nothing else. He pumped gas, a man of forty-five. He was night watchman at a lumberyard. He tried all kinds of things, but nothing worked out."

"I remember," said Emily.

"No you don't! And every time he went down into Lake Hills, he got crazy. Seeing all those rich people. He'd get into trouble, too. Fights. Too much drinking in the bars. He thought everybody was laughing at him because we were from the hills and dirt poor. It drove him crazy."

I felt a chill. That was Adam's thing, about people laughing. Could it go from father to son, like green eyes or freckles? Maybe; I don't know; I'm no expert.

"Well, *I'm* not laughing," I said. "I like Adam and I like you and Emily, and I—believe me—I have nothing to do with that other stuff."

"Oh, I was just talking, honey. I have a big mouth. Of course you don't have nothing to do with it. But can you see me spending the rest of my life in a mobile home? Little tiny rooms and a concrete block—that's your porch—and half a tree and two geraniums and some gravel—that's your garden. Not me! Maybe this place isn't much, but I can get myself up in the morning and I can see eighteen miles out that way, and I can spot fifteen, twenty different kinds of birds, and I can spit right out the back window if I want, and nobody can tell me *nothing*! We own this place, and we are not moving one inch! You show your pictures of how good we live here, and how we *do* for ourselves and care about each other, and maybe some people will see. Those pictures of them muffins you took, that's good. There isn't one woman down in Lake Hills who knows how to make real corn muffins from real corn-meal and real butter and real eggs! They buy the boxes in those stores with music in all the aisles.''

My home-ec eccentric mother is a terrific cook, if nothing else, and she bakes up a storm sometimes—maybe not corn muffins, but bread and cakes and pies—all from scratch. She has these all-day baking binges. But I wasn't about to mention this to Mrs. Bates.

''I'd give anything if my pictures could do some good,'' I said. I meant it.

''Oh, they will, honey! They will! People are afraid to come up here. Now they can see we aren't two-headed monsters. You ought to take some pictures of the Koerners' house down the road a half mile. Why don't you take her, Adam?''

''Oh, uh— No thank you, Mrs. Bates. I just wanted

121

to do one house really well. I have more than enough shots now."

"No, you don't," said Emily, looking hurt. "You didn't take none of my room."

"Oh. I didn't?"

"No. You took Adam's room, and Ma's room, and the kitchen, and the yucky outhouse, but not my room."

"Okay. You must be right," I said. "Well, I've got some film left. Let's do your room now, okay?"

"Yaah! Good-iee!" Emily shouted.

I took my equipment into Emily's room, while Adam helped his mother clean out the oven. Emily had a mattress right on the dirt floor, just like Adam did in his room, and a beat-up old dressing table, and a big crate full of wrecked toys. She started posing by the little window, and that, of course, was all wrong for what I was doing. I tried to get her to be nice and natural again, but I just couldn't. She was being giggly and was sort of teasing me, as if I should try and catch her being normal. So I started to shoot things in the room: first her mattress, then her dressing table. I focused in on the top of her table to capture all the mess of stuff there—just like my desk top—moved in a little closer, focused again, and . . .

And I froze. I *froze*! There on her dressing table, almost hidden behind a purse, was— I was dreaming;

122

it *couldn't* be. A crystal paperweight. It had to be one of my mother's. It *was* one of my mother's. I knew that paperweight! I went over and studied it. I felt sick.

The red and blue swirling lines buried in the glass met and crisscrossed and ended in a sprig of tiny white flowers. I turned it over. On the bottom was a little gold label with the number 103 in red ink. My mother had numbered every paperweight so she could organize and keep track of her collection.

I felt *sick*!

How, how could he *do* this! What was wrong with him! He was a thief!

He couldn't have done it! I felt a sliver of hope. He couldn't have. Impossible. He was never alone in the living room, last week at my house. How? Oh, no. The bathroom. He'd gone to the bathroom. There were shelves with paperweights on display in the . . .

Oh, this was it! This was it! The end! Good-bye Adam! Mom had been right! As usual. I felt absolutely sick. Sick to my stomach. Sick at heart. Sick at the world.

"Em . . . Emily," I said shakily, "where did you get this from?"

"Adam gave me it. It was a present. Isn't it beautiful? You want to take a picture of it?"

"Yes," I said. "No. No . . . Emily, could I . . . I want to talk to Adam in your room. Alone. Please?"

123

"Okay." She was very serious now. I must have looked like a Halloween ghost. "Should I call him?"

"Pl-please call him, Emily."

"Why are you crying?"

"Please. Emily. Please. Just . . . just tell him I want to talk to him."

"Okay."

Adam came in after a moment, and he was smiling. He was smiling! Emily must have said something, because he knew what it was about. "I was going to t-tell you," he said. "But I forgot. She likes it. She c-carries it with her everywhere."

"You . . . *forgot*?"

"I f-forgot to tell you."

"You . . ." I couldn't say it. I just wanted to run. "You st . . . You stole one of my mother's paper-weights."

"No. No, I *took* it."

"You stole it!"

"I t-took it. To show Emily."

"You mean—you were going to bring it back?"

"No. Can't Emily have it?"

"I don't— I can't believe— How could you take something like this from my house! How *could* you!" I was trying to keep my voice down, but I was ready to scream.

124

"You got so many."

"They're not mine! They're my mother's! And they're antiques! You—I can't believe you! You could have asked. You *should* have asked. You're a—you're a thief!"

"But Emily doesn't have an-anything! She . . . look at that junk she's got in that box. She's g-got nothing but junk. And your mother has so much. And Emily, she never had anything like this in her whole life. And she likes it so m-much! Where I come from, people give people things, like gifts. People can take something, and it's n-not stealing, because they know that you would want them to have it. On Vega-X people g-give people everything. On Vega-X—"

"No more! I don't want to hear any more of your Vega-X garbage! You use it for every stupid thing you do! You use it as an excuse for everything! There is no Vega-X, and you know it! This is too much, Adam! I want out! I can't handle it!"

I gathered all my camera gear and carried it out to my bike in the front yard. Adam followed me. Mrs. Bates tried to say something as I rushed through the kitchen, but I didn't give her a chance.

"But . . . no," Adam said. "Lisa, no. You d-don't understand! On Vega-X—"

"*No!*"

125

"P-people give— There *is* a Vega-X—and people g-give—"

"I've got to go, Adam." I jammed my cameras and junk into the pannier on my bike, and stuffed the paperweight in also. "And I'm taking this back. It's my mother's—and you stole it—and I'm taking it back."

"L-lisa . . ." His head was down.

"Adam. Look at me! If you had asked . . . If you had told me you wanted one for Emily, there could have been a way, maybe. I could have gotten one, somehow . . ." I mounted the bike, ready to shove off.

"I'm sorry, Lisa."

"Adam, what's the use! If you'll do this, you'll do anything! You'll—you'll steal a camera. Because you don't have one, and I have three. What's the use! I can't trust you. You'll say Vega-X, and *whammo*, everything's okay. Well, it's not! It's not! *This* is the world you have to live in, not Vega-X. What's the use?"

"Lisa . . ." He was crying now.

"I've got to go, Adam."

"I'm s-sorry. I'm sorry . . ."

"Let me cool down. Let me go home. I've got to think. Let me go home."

"I w-won't do it again . . . I swear." He stood in

126

front of my bike, blocking my way. "You're the only f-friend I have."

"Adam, please! Don't do this to me! You're tearing me apart! You are! Why can't you just be a plain louse! Adam, I've got to go! Get out of my way!"

"Okay . . . You're just like all the r-rest."

"I guess I am. I'm a human being. From planet *Earth*!"

"I came from Vega! I came f-from—"

"I don't believe you."

"I did. And I didn't s-steal it!"

"I've got to think! Say good-bye to Emily and your mother for me. I'll probably see you—around—in school."

"G-good-bye."

"Good-bye . . . Adam."

We were both crying now. Adam and me both. Shit! I pushed off and pedaled and careened down that stupid rutted road and nearly broke my neck.

I wished I had.

12

WHEN MOM SAW my face as I charged into the house
she put her hand up to her mouth. I'd been blurry-eyed
all the way home on my bike. Lucky I didn't hit a car.

"Lisa, what is it?"

"I'm okay, Mom. Little problem. Just leave me be!
Please!"

"Did that boy do something to you. . . ."

"No! I'm okay. I just want to be alone in my room.
Please!"

"All right. All right."

I dropped my bike pannier on the floor of my room,

fell onto my bed face forward, and cried till my pillow was slimy with my tears and snot. During this, Mom came in very quietly, put her hand on my arm, and kissed me on the back of my head. I cried all over again. Then, to her everlasting credit, she quietly walked out. She seemed to know what I'd needed then, and it helped. A lot. I guess Mom's been there, too. I guess everybody has.

I lay on my bed for a little while longer, numbed-out from all the crying, feeling totally miserable. Why did I care so much? I'd only known him for a week. He was just another boy; why did I care? I shouldn't have. It was stupid. But I did. I'd gotten myself hooked. I loved his stammer —I couldn't help it—I did! And his gentleness. And his shyness. I loved his way of shrugging. And his quirky brightness. And his face. And his hair. And his arms. Everything.

I am a jerk. I am.

As I began to return to a kind of sad reality, I suddenly sat up. The paperweight! Dumb! The first thing to do was to put that paperweight back, no matter what! All I needed was for Mom to discover it missing. So far she hadn't.

I put the paperweight in my jeans pocket but it made too big a lump, so I put it into my shower cap, wrapped the shower cap in my bathrobe, and went down the

129

hall to the bathroom. And, of course, the door was locked; Mom had gotten there first.

Logic told me that if she hadn't noticed all weekend, she probably wouldn't notice the missing paperweight now. More logic told me that she usually used the bathroom connected to the master bedroom—Mom and Dad's bedroom—when she was upstairs, and not *this* one, which was for guests and for me, so she might not yet have had a close encounter of the first kind with the missing paperweight. But she was in there and I was out here, and I was panicking.

"Mom? Will you be out soon?"

"Are you okay now?" she called to me.

"I'm fine! I want to take a shower!"

"Oh, you can use *our* bathroom."

"No. I like this one."

"What? Why?"

"The shower is . . . better! It's more pin-pointy."

"I'll be right out."

"Thanks."

I pictured her examining the paperweights, one by one. Was there a gap on the shelves, like a tooth knocked out, where paperweight 103 had been? Oh, was I getting tense.

"Mom?"

"Yes! In a minute!"

130

Tense, tense, tense. I began to kick myself for my crying jag before; if I hadn't buried myself in my room Mom wouldn't have come upstairs, and if she hadn't come up, she would have used the little bathroom right off the kitchen. We have a very well-toileted house— four, count them, four—including the one we converted into a darkroom. I guess this huge barn of a house had been intended for a family of fifty.

Mom finally came out and I slipped by her and charged into the bathroom to avoid a third degree on my recent hysteria.

"Lisa, are you all—"

"I'm fine now, Mother!"

"But what hap—"

"Nothing, Mom. Everything's okay." I shut the door.

"Why are you showering in the middle of the afternoon?" she called through the door. The third degree was on, like it or not.

"I took all those photos, and when I do that I work up a sweat, Mom." Which, by the way, is true.

"What happened at that boy's house?"

"Mother, his name is Adam. And nothing happened."

I examined the shelf while we spoke. Yes, there was a gap! Third shelf down. How could she have missed it? How could *I* have missed it? But I had. I'd lucked out on this one. I put the paperweight back and adjusted it to be in line with the others.

"If nothing happened, why are you taking a shower?" Mom called through the door again. She refused to quit.

"Oh, Mom, please!"

"Well . . . You're absolutely sure you're all right?"

"Yes, Mom! Yes!"

I turned on the shower full blast, to drown out further questions. And I must say, I really enjoyed it. Showers can be mind altering at the right time. I showered for a shameless twenty minutes, trying not to think about Adam, and as a result, thought about him the entire time.

Why, *why* did I still care about him? Why did I visualize scenes of his coming over to me in school tomorrow telling me how sorry he was, and how the planet Vega-X story was all baloney, and how he was going to join our community swim team, and join the world, and how he liked me so much—so very much—and, in fact, loved me? Why was I such a grade-B sentimental boob?

I felt better after the shower, more in control, more my own person, more self-contained, or whatever the appropriate bull words are. But I was still confused and troubled about Adam. One part of me was angry and hurt while another part was feeling, somewhere deep down, that if I'd been poor and kicked around, and had been in Adam's shoes, with Emily as my sister, maybe I would have done the same thing. But a third part—I have millions of parts when I get going—a third part felt that I couldn't trust Adam for anything. That it wasn't just that paperweight; there were other things, too. That he was weird, or sick, or unstable, or possibly even dangerous, and that you can't fight the way the world is, and that Mom, maybe, was right. And Kim, too. There was even a small, selfish part of me saying: there goes the photo contest. Because I wasn't going to go ahead with that anymore, for sure. Eight rolls of film down the drain.

And then, back in my room, I saw Adam's wilted flower and his note and I got this huge lump at the bottom of my throat, and I felt the old tears streaming again. Some self-contained!

It was bad. I'd sunk all the way down again. I'm afraid I may be closer to Mom than I'd like, with these sudden mood shifts and reversals. Anyway, it was bad. I had to talk to someone; I couldn't get my head straight. I was going up and down like a yo-yo.

Kim and I have a sort of password that we'd invented in fifth grade. If we ever had a really serious problem, something urgent, we'd just say *emergency squad*, and we'd drop whatever we were doing, even if we were in the middle of a school day, or dinner, or anything, and get over and help the other guy. So far, neither of us had ever used it. I wasn't sure that Kim even remembered anymore. But I got on the phone and called her.

"Emergency squad," I said, loud and clear, when she got on.

"Emergency squad?" she asked.

"Right. Emergency squad," I repeated.

"I'm on my way."

From the click of the receiver to her appearance at our front door, I counted three minutes and forty seconds. And she's a six-minute bike ride away.

That's Kim.

13

I TOLD KIM about everything: Vega-X, the stolen paperweight, Adam's scarred back—the works. I talked and talked, sprawled out there on the floor beside her, almost as if I was thinking out loud. Is that what it's like to go to a shrink?

Kim was wonderful; she hardly said a word while I rambled on. A few *oh, wows* at the right places, some *uh huhs* to keep me going, but not once did she tell me that she'd warned me. Not a single *I told you so*, my mother's battle cry.

It felt good unloading the burden; I think I'd been

135

feeling completely disoriented, trying to fall into step with Adam's strangeness while keeping it all to myself. Somewhere I'd heard this called *folie à deux*—craziness of two—where, if one person of a couple is bananas, the other can start thinking it's perfectly normal and go bananas, too. Kim was so sane and practical; just having her next to me made me feel back on solid ground.

"So you've had a learning experience," said Kim, my little mother of the moment. "That's the way to look at it. I'm treating Russ as a learning experience, basically. It's no big deal. Almost nobody ends up with the person they went with at fourteen, anyway. What do you know at fourteen? What do I know? Nothing. Face it. I didn't even know which artery takes blood away from the left ventricle of the heart on that lousy test. So how can I know what my heart's pitter-pattering over? The same goes for you. Right?"

Kim had never been this sensible before about herself, Russ, or anyone. She'd been thinking about this a lot, I could tell.

"I guess so," I said. "But I still like Adam. That's the problem."

"So what. I still like Russ, even though . . . nothing."

"What?" The spotlight moved from me to her. What was all this about Russ?

"Nothing."

"Kimberly! I've told you everything about Adam, maybe too much! Because I swore not to tell anybody. I trust *you*. Don't you think you can trust *me*?"

"Okay . . . It's no big deal. Not like with Adam. It's, well, he's been saying he doesn't want to go out with me anymore unless we you-know-what. And I said, no way, José. And he keeps threatening to split, and I keep saying no, and it's driving me bats."

"Do you want to you-know-what?"

"No! Come on, Lee!"

"Then don't."

"I'm having trouble keeping his paws off me. You saw him at the beach, and that was like nothing. What really bothers me is, I think he just wants to impress his friends. I think he's acting like this because he's supposed to."

"I wouldn't be so sure of that."

"Lee, do you know that he writes poetry?"

"*Russ?*"

"Yes! He does! Lousy poetry, but it's still poetry. I mean there's this other side of him that he's so afraid of. He told me to swear not to tell anybody. Including you. So now we've both told things we swore not to tell. When does the bolt of lightning strike?"

"Now!" I said. *"Zzabam!"* I thumped her with a pillow from my bed.

137

"That hurts, Lisa! Anyway, I'm just hanging in there with Russ. It's not bad. I'm getting really good at twisting out of his reach."

"You can overdo that, too," I said.

"What?"

"Twisting out of reach. There *are* happy compromises, Kim."

"I know that, Lee Lee. I wasn't born yesterday. But we have to take care of your problem, not mine. I think you ought to let the whole thing with Adam end quietly. You're no shrink; you can't straighten him out. He needs a shrink, Lisa. He's got too many problems. I mean, good grief, planet Varga and—"

"Vega."

"And stealing and everything. Lee, there aren't enough hours in the day. . . . It'll only hurt him more, and you, too, if you stay and stay and finally have to break up anyway." More sensible advice. Kim was really with it today.

"You're right," I said. "When you're right, you're right. Okay! Okay! That's it! Mom will be in seventh heaven."

"Never mind your mother. You have to do what's right for you."

"Okay. I agree."

Just then, as if we were connected by mental telepathy waves, Mom called up to me for dinner. I'd heard Dad come in before, but it hadn't really registered.

"Kim, please," I said, "stay for dinner. If you're there my mother won't work me over with a million stupid questions."

"But I already ate."

"Force yourself!"

"I don't know," she said, trying to get a rise out of me. "It depends. What's on the menu?"

"Chicken, I think."

"Hmm. Fried?"

"My mother frying chicken! You must be mad! It's chicken marsala or coq au vin, at least!"

"Well, *perhaps* I'll stay."

"Perhaps, huh?"

"Perhaps."

"Good!" Then I shouted down the stairs in my carnival-barker voice, "Mom, can Kim stay for dinner? Please?"

"Yes!" Mom's voice rose back up. "Certainly!" Mom sounded happy. Her daughter had been saved. She knew what was going on; she can read minds. First, daughter home in tears. Then the purifying shower. Then the supportive friend who loves flowers, Kim the Capable, appears on the scene. Next, friend stays for

139

dinner on a cheery note. Conclusion: one problem boy-friend dumped. Mom knew. Well, at least someone was made happy by this whole mess.

I'd been right for a change; the dinner went smoothly, with Dad explaining and, in fact, sort of showing off to Kim about how a TV ad is produced. Poor Kim—she'd heard it all before. But she did have seconds of Mom's chicken, so it wasn't a total loss.

During the lemon cake, I announced that I had mountains of homework—which was true; I always have mountains of homework—to allow me to disappear safely into my room and evade that third degree. Kim came up to my room for another half hour or so, and repeated the logic, once more, of letting the Adam connection disconnect. She added a few new points, which I would just as soon have done without.

"There are plenty of guys out there, Lee, who I know would like you if you gave them half a chance. It isn't as if Adam is the only human boy in North Jersey."

"Oh, really? And how do I give them a chance?"

"Do the things I showed you for your eyes and hair and all. And hang around. Go down to the beach. And the handball court. They always hang around the handball court. And the volleyball court."

"Oh, *those* guys. Russ's buddies. Thanks a lot, Kim.

But you'd better give me some twisting-out-of-reach lessons first.''

"Some of those guys are very nice. Are you going to use what I told you about Russ and me against me now?''

"No. I'm sorry, Kim. That wasn't fair. But I'm not going to just hang around. I have to really, really like somebody. Okay? I really liked Adam. He could have been great. . . .''

"I know you liked him, Lee. I know you did. You'll be okay. You bounce back all the time. I've seen it.''

"That's me. The human Ping-Pong ball.''

"You'll be okay,'' Kim repeated.

"Thanks for coming over, Kim. I think my head is on straight now. Thanks.''

"No problem. The chicken was worth it.''

"I saw you gorge yourself, Miss Piggy.''

"Polite people never notice.''

"Who says I'm polite? I was going to get my camera and take some pictures.''

As we said good-bye at the door I gave Kim a huge bear hug. It was nice and warm, but after she left I felt empty. Maybe I needed a hug, myself, just then from someone. From Dad. Or Mom. Or Adam. Or Grandpa. If he were here, I know he would have said the right thing. But what? I felt empty, almost the way

141

I feel after throwing up. I had "thrown up" Adam and whatever we'd had between us. . . .

I did my homework, some low hills if not mountains of it, listened to a couple of my tapes, including an old Sarah Vaughan that made my eyes get blurry, showered again, forgetting I'd showered before, and went to bed. The big decision had been made. It was over.

14

I LAY THERE in bed turning left, then right, then left again, for a solid hour. Every time I thought of Adam, I tried to push him out of my mind, like one of those Zen meditation exercises I'd read about. *Blank*. Think *blank*. Or say *Om*. But after a short while his face would reappear on my mental video screen, with his sad eyes and shy mouth. Then the action would begin again, like a freeze-frame unfreezing. I pictured him running into the lake to save that kid. I saw him swinging Emily. I watched him pass his note with that flower to me again. And again. And again. Think *blank*. Think *blank*.

I heard Mom and Dad come upstairs, murmur something in the hallway, and close their bedroom door. I could hear the soft whoosh of their shower going, reflected in the pipes of the bathroom next to my bedroom. If there was water running anywhere in the house, you could hear it anywhere else, when it was quiet at night. I heard the larger ghost sound of their toilet flushing and thought of Adam's outhouse. Again, Adam! I pictured him—I am not embarrassed—sitting there in that smelly outhouse. It didn't seem fair. What had I done to deserve four bathrooms? What had he done to deserve none? Why him? Why me?

It started me thinking about children I'd seen on TV, some close to skeletons they were so thin, starving in Africa. What had I done to deserve chicken marsala and homemade lemon cake? Been born lucky? Grandpa always used to say: you've been born lucky; now use it! I felt almost as if we were talking, he and I. Well, someday I hoped to use my photojournalism to help the unlucky; to photograph them and show the world. To report the truth. That was the real Lisa Daniels, the me in me that I knew was there, hidden but ready, like an exposed film waiting to be developed.

Hold on, I thought. The time to begin is now! Grandpa used to say that too. Well he was right! If I was going to be a photojournalist, the real stuff, it had to start

144

now. This very minute! Those pictures of Adam were going up!

I put my jeans back on, and my T-shirt, grabbed my bag of exposed film and went down the hallway to bathroom *numero cuatro*, the darkroom. I took the developing tank and reels off the shelf, and the timer and bottle of developer. I was getting excited now; I felt the way I feel on a diving board, looking down into the bottomless pool. As I poured the developer into a beaker, my hands felt a little trembly. Why was I so nervous? I've been anxious about my photos coming out right before, but this was something else. It was because of Adam, I knew. But it was over between us. Over!

I made up the stop bath and fixer in two more beakers, got my first two rolls of film and turned out the light. I popped open the film cartridges with a beer can opener, loaded the reels by touch in the dark, put the reels back in the tank, then filled and rinsed once with plain water. It was something Dad had taught me to do to get rid of air bubbles and prevent streaks.

Then I took my usual deep breath and got ready for the start of the race. I poured in the developer and set the timer going the instant I poured. I closed the tank, banged it down against the sink to get rid of bubbles, then turned on the light. Then I agitated the tank my

145

own special way, back and forth as if casting a witch's spell, counting to five each time, then banged the tank for air bubbles again.

If only life could be as simple as developing film. In developing, if you do everything right, things will generally come out okay. In life, read that as *my* life, the more I try the more I seem to mess up.

The timer was a few seconds from buzzing, so I got set to pour out the developer. To me this was always the most hectic moment. Out went the developer into a beaker, in went the stop bath. I started the timer again, and did some more agitating. Next came the fixer. Then the water rinse. And finally, at last, the film.

As I lifted the first strip of wet film gently out of its reel, I could see things were good. Very good. I don't need contact prints to see what I have; I can read negatives like the blind read braille. I turn things right side up in my head: dark to light, light to dark. And I could see at a glance as I hung up the film that all was well with my shining wet necklace of black and white jewels, bright and sparkling. I examined it as I slowly wiped it down, down with my two sponges, front and back. I studied my ghost world of Adam and Emily and Mrs. Bates and the house and the windows and the junk pile, all reversed: the dark sky, the white

146

trees, Emily floating weightless in the air, hanging from Adam's outstretched ghost hands, as if they were underwater. There was Vega-X, right there!

But I made my contact prints, of course. Contacts, I should explain, are made directly from the negatives, with no enlargement, for checking purposes. And I'd been right; they were wonderful. *Adam* was wonderful; his eyes, even in those tiny photos, looked shy and hurt, yet loving. Oh, Adam! You stupid jerk!

It's one thing to be torn once. But here I was, the Lake Hills idiot, being torn apart—twice! It was as if Adam were right next to me, holding my hand, talking to me. *L-lisa.* His voice was in my ear as I worked.

And did I work! I developed, and fixed, and wiped, and made prints until three-thirty A.M. *L-lisa.*

Yes, friends, you guessed it. Sorry Kim. Sorry Mom. Sorry. It wasn't quite over yet. I wasn't going to give up yet. Not yet. Adam and I were going to have a long, long talk tomorrow. At lunch. Or right after school. About Vega-X, and paperweights, and shoes and ships and sealing wax, and cabbages and kings. A very serious talk. About us.

15

I WENT TO school that next morning full of speeches I'd prepared about forgiveness and renewal. I was dead tired from last night's photo marathon; I had to direct myself, step by step, through the labyrinth of the day. *Now you get off the bus. Now you go, yes, to homeroom. That's right.*

In homeroom, I told Kim of my new reversal and warned her to not rock my boat since I was a walking zombie from sleep deprivation.

"I knew you'd change your mind," she said sweetly.

Only to me, with my heavy eyes and brain, it sounded

148

like sarcasm. In a way, it's not bad being tired; your reaction time to cute remarks, real or imagined, is so slow that the remarks just float by you like so many puffs of smoke.

Anyway, I had my words all prepared for Adam. My emotions, too. I was going to be very calm and collected, no matter what. Not like my hysterical outburst yesterday. I was ready. The only problem was, Adam wasn't in school. He didn't show up for science class. No one had seen him in the halls. He wasn't in the cafeteria. He wasn't anywhere.

My speeches shriveled up in my brain. I had been ready for everything—from Adam being angry to his behaving as if nothing had happened—but I hadn't expected this. Was he out sick? Or was he out because of our fight? And if it *was* because of our fight, wasn't that a sign of instability in itself?

My anxiety level started rising; I found it hard to concentrate on the math being flung out at us by Mr. Weber. It was kind of psycho; there I was half asleep, yet I kept getting these little jolts of anxiety every time I thought of Adam. If only he hadn't looked so hurt when we'd split yesterday. I recalled his face again, with those angry tears, and his words: *You're just like all the rest.* Was that hurt, or was that anger? At the time I'd felt it as anger, but now I wasn't so sure. It was hurt. Or anger covering hurt . . . but it had all been his fault!

And so it went all day at school. I was playing tennis against myself, back and forth, back and forth. A good way to go nuts. I decided I'd phone him the moment I got home. Maybe we could arrange to meet down at the library and talk things out. And maybe I'd bring the contact prints with me. A good idea. It might break the ice and get us on the right track again.

But, when I got home at three, there was a new problem. I was so numb I'd completely forgotten— Adam didn't have a phone! End of plan A.

My mind was going blank. I had to crash into my bed for a nap or I'd fall asleep standing up. I made a new decision: I'd wait till tomorrow, one more day. If Adam wasn't in school tomorrow, I'd bike up to his house after school.

As I lay on top of the covers, half asleep, I made another decision: I'd set my alarm for half an hour, then get up and start working on my final prints, the enlargements for the contest. That was always one of the joys of photography to me: selecting the good shots and blowing them up to full life. But, of course, I fell asleep before I could set the alarm. I slept for almost four hours. Mom, mercifully, didn't wake me. And more merciful yet, she and Dad had to go out that evening, so when I awoke, there was no chance for the inquisition I'd successfully avoided so far. As they went out the door, I went downstairs. There were notes all over the kitchen telling me what to warm up for dinner, what to not throw out, and where they had gone, complete with phone number. I felt as if Mom was making me into my own babysitter, at fourteen. Good old Mom; she'll never grow up.

I think Mom was on a new approach with me, now that the Adam crisis was over, in her mind. She hadn't asked me anything at breakfast, I realized, not even why I looked so tired. My guess was that it was something she'd read in one of her magazines. You know the scene: *Leave them alone and they'll tell you. All in good time. Don't push. Keep the lines of communication open. And make sure they aren't stealing from your purse.*

Wide awake and recovered now, I gorged on warmed-over lasagna, did my homework in the record time of half an hour, then went on an enlargement binge.

Dad found me in the darkroom at one A.M., my head down on the sink, asleep, with only the yellow safelight on, and my glorious glossy enlargements all over the place. When he woke me up gently, he said, "Sweets, these pictures are great. Someday, I'm going to say I knew you when . . . Is that your friend Adam there? The boy in those photos?"

"Yes," I said, my eyes half closed.

151

"You know . . . I think I like him," he said, examining the prints. "Whatever your problems are—Mom told me you've been crying—if we can help, let us know."

"Thanks, Dad."

"Now, get to bed—before I cancel your darkroom privileges for the next thirty-six years."

16

ADAM WAS OUT the next day, too. I felt a hollowness inside, as if some vital organ were missing. I remember feeling that way after Grandpa died. I'd expect Grandpa to walk in any minute, just as he used to do, with his coffee mug in one hand and his newspaper in the other. And now, in that same way, I kept looking around for Adam, hoping to see him come down the hall or into the classroom. Suddenly there.

I purposely went by the Resource Room between classes, to have a look. Mrs. Gladdings was outside the door, on hall duty. Would she know why he was

153

out? All kinds of questions spun in my head as I walked over; Mrs. Gladdings must know plenty about Adam. But the bell had rung and she was going back into her room.

"Oh, Mrs. Gladdings," I said. "Excuse me. Uh—could I talk to you for a minute?"

"Not right now. I have a class. Don't you?" she said, looking me over. Did she know who I was, I wondered.

"Well, could I talk to you sometime when you're free?"

"I'll be free at the end of the lunch hour. I'll be right here in the room. How's that?"

"Oh, that's fine."

"What's this all about?"

"Uh, Adam. Adam Bates."

"Oh, yes. I've seen you with him, haven't I?" Right on target. She must watch over her flock all the time.

"Oh . . . Uh, yes!"

"Lisa? Aren't you Lisa?"

"Yes." She knew my name, probably from Adam. It felt funny. I had been talked about.

"I was just wondering, Lisa . . . Is Adam in some kind of trouble?"

"No. No."

"Oh. Well, that's a relief."

154

I rattled around the rest of the morning, not really knowing what I was doing. I'd brought in samples of the big glossy prints and all the small contact prints to show Adam. They were in my backpack, between stiff cardboard, and before every class I checked to see that they weren't getting wrecked. That was my major accomplishment.

I showed the prints to Kim in the cafeteria. She thought they were great, terrific, fabulous. But her words of praise didn't register on me; all during lunch I was thinking of Adam and my questions for Mrs. Gladdings.

Near the end of the hour, I went over to the Resource Room. Mrs. Gladdings motioned to me to sit down by her desk. She looked worried. What did she think I was going to say?

"Well, Lisa," she began, "I have a cafeteria doughnut here. Would you like half?"

"Oh, no thanks, Mrs.Gladdings. Uh, what I wanted to ask was, do you have any idea why Adam's out today?"

"No, I don't. I was wondering if *you* knew."

"Well, I don't know if he's out sick, or if—" I didn't want to mention our fight, so I skirted it. "Or if it's . . . Well, he's got lots of problems, right?"

"Oh, I suppose. . . . Yes," she said, hesitantly. I

155

guess I wasn't supposed to ask.

"But he's really bright, isn't he? I mean, he reads everything in the library."

"Oh, he's very bright," she said. "But . . . well . . . his problems are masking the brightness, if you see what I mean."

"Uh huh. Would you know if he's ever seen a psychologist or anything?" I asked.

"Lisa, come on! I can't discuss that."

"Please? I'm just trying to understand things. I really like Adam. I really do. Please?"

"Well . . . This will *not* go any further, right? Counseling was suggested to his mother, but she doesn't believe in psychologists. There's just so much we can do in the school. It's a shame."

"You can't tell me what any of his problems are, can you?"

"You know I can't. If you know Adam, you should guess some of them. Have you every been up to his house?"

"Yes." The first bell sounded. I should have come earlier.

"My kids are going to be piling in here any minute, Lisa. Let me just say . . . I think Adam can use a good friend like you. But, he has problems."

I took a stab in the dark. "Like Vega-X?" I asked.

156

"I don't understand," she said. She didn't know about it.

"Can't you tell me, at least, why he was put in our science class so late in the year? Was he being main-streamed?"

"No, he was in a different science class before. Certain students harassed him. I'm really stretching the rules, but . . . The teacher couldn't handle it. Adam needs a very firm teacher, like Mrs. Felts."

"Oh, I see. Mrs. Gladdings, I swear, I'm not going to spread anything. Couldn't you tell me a little more? Because I hardly know anything. Adam doesn't talk and I . . . Please?"

"Well, let me think. . . . I guess it's no secret. Did you know that, in grade school, Adam fought all the time? He hurt a few boys quite badly. One had his nose broken. And a tooth knocked out. His parents called the police. Adam has a very quick temper; he ignites. But I think, I hope, he's been controlling it. He hasn't fought with anyone, to my knowledge, since early in seventh grade. Does that help?"

"Yes. Yes. Thank you."

"I like Adam. He's got a lot of good stuff in him. I wish I could help you and Adam. But I just can't say any more."

"I—I know he was beaten by his father," I said.

157

"Good! I'm glad you know that, because *that* I couldn't tell you. I'm sorry, Lisa. I hope this helps a little. . . ."

Broken nose! Tooth knocked out! Oh, brother! Hadn't I seen him struggling with himself on the school bus? And with Russ on the beach? He seemed to blank out when kids made fun of him. No reaction. None. Because, if he'd reacted, he would have gone bonkers, I guess. Was this a new problem, or part of the old problems? I didn't know, but I was getting worried again. *I think Adam can use a good friend like you.* And I'd just about broken up with him.

Well, Mrs. Gladdings was not going to scare me off, not that she'd intended to. Or had she? Either way, I was more and more determined to have one last go-for-broke try with Adam that afternoon.

When I got home after school, I first raided the refrigerator, as usual. My raids are healthy though: milk, a plum, and one single, solitary cookie, nibbled slowly. I went into the living room; Mom seemed to still be glowing from my presumed breakup with Adam. She had a friend over, and she was actually bubbling.

"Hello, Lisa!" she called. "My favorite scholar! And how was Lake Hills Middle School today?"

"Putrid," I said. "Smellorama." I guess I was thinking about Adam being out. Mom looked at her friend, Mrs. Freeman, more than a little embarrassed.

"Lovely. So nice to hear good things," Mom said. "Going over to Kim's?"

"No, Adam's," I answered. Poor Mom. Maybe I should have done a half lie and said *I don't know; I guess*, then told her the bad news later. Anyway, her face fell about a foot.

"Adam? But, I thought . . . well . . . Is everything—all right?"

"I hope so."

Mrs. Freeman nodded and smiled and said, "Kids. The more you try, the less you can keep up with them." Very profound.

"Oh, by the way," I said, "I just saw Joshua on the way home from school and I think his pants are ripped." Joshua is Mrs. Freeman's son; I guess I mentioned him before. Of course, I hadn't seen him; I was just entertaining Mom a little. Yes, it was mean; Mom had been darn nice this last day or so. But I didn't like the way her expression changed when I'd mentioned Adam, as if she'd bitten into a charcoal-broiled pickle.

"Well, that's Joshua," said Mrs. Freeman nonchalantly, with a you-can't-bother-me smile. I'd deserved it. Joshua had just won some incredible chess tournament—I mean serious chess—and he's only sixteen, if that. I guess he's a genius. Well, maybe Adam

159

is, too, Mother, if you'd give him half a chance! And what if he isn't? What if he's just a good decent person like Dad? Or you? Or me? On second thought, cancel me.

Anyway, I'd caused a disruption in the airwaves, so to speak, with Mom and Mrs. Freeman trying to diplomatically ignore the last two minutes as if they had never happened. Sometimes I am a scuzz bomb.

I put all the prints, protected by the cardboard, into the pannier on my bike and headed toward the hills. I tried to not think as I biked; thinking would tense me up all over again. I rode. And I rode. Going over to Adam's house is very good exercise, I must say. By the time I was bobbling over the ruts toward his front yard, I was totally pooped.

Emily was out front with a friend, a girl about her age. I'd wondered if she ever had anyone in the world to play with besides Adam.

"Cathy, it's Lisa! Look! Lisa, hi! Lisa, hi! Hi!"

I was really glad to see Emily. She ran over to me, and I got off the bike and hugged her. By this time, Mrs. Bates was at the front door.

"Why, Lisa, honey! Hello there! Hello!"

"Hi, Mrs. Bates," I said, walking my bike over to her. "I, uh, is Adam inside?"

"Why, no. I don't know where he is. Maybe he's

160

still at the school. Or the library. He's always at that library."

She didn't know he'd been out of school. Oh, wow. Something was wrong, for sure. Emily was tugging at me, but I wasn't in the mood for playing.

"Well," I said, "I guess I'll bike down and try the library."

"Oh, come in and have some milk first," said Mrs. Bates. "Emily! Stop pulling Lisa's belt!"

"I wanna talk to her."

"Play with Cathy."

"I wanna talk to her."

"Well, talk then! I'll get some milk and cookies." As Mrs. Bates disappeared into the house Emily pulled me down toward her, so she could whisper in my ear. Cathy had come close to listen. Emily turned to her for a second and said, like any twenty-two-year-old, "Cathy, this is private!" Then she whispered to me, "I'm sorry about the paperweight, Lisa."

"That's okay," I said. "It wasn't your fault."

"Adam's up at that open field on the way to the capsule place. He went there yesterday, too. Don't tell Ma."

I knew the field she meant. The place where he went to think. Oh, feet, carry me there fast! He *had* been brooding. He *had* been hurt.

161

But Mrs. Bates wouldn't let me go. She was back at the door with a dish of homemade gingersnaps. "Come on, Lisa," she said. "Don't be bashful, honey."

"I—I'd really like to catch Adam."

"Oh, he'll be home soon. His stomach knows the way toward supper. Please come in, honey. I want to talk to you a minute."

It sounded serious. Okay, I thought. Maybe I'd learn something. I went in, with Emily and Cathy right behind me.

"Not you, Emily! There's milk on the table. You and Cathy get your milk and your gingersnaps and take them outside. Hear now!"

When we were alone, Mrs. Bates eased herself onto one of the rickety kitchen chairs and gestured to me to take another.

"There," she said. "Oh, I'm so glad you're here. I'm so glad. What happened, day before yesterday? You were taking all those pictures and everything was so nice, and then suddenly you and Adam were shouting and—and he's crying and you're crying, and you go and rush off."

"Didn't Adam tell you anything?" I asked.

"No. All he said was you had a fight. That's all."

"But didn't Emily say anything?"

"She says she doesn't know. 'I don't know. I don't

know.' That's all she says. But then, she and Adam never tell me anything, anyway.''

"Well . . . We did have an argument. But I've come to try to, you know, straighten it out.''

"I'm so glad. Adam likes you so much. We all do. Oh, honey, I'm scared it's what I said to you. About charity, and your prize money, and the folks down in Lake Hills. I wouldn't hurt or insult you for the world. Or Adam—I wouldn't say anything to hurt him; he's been hurt so bad, so many times.''

"I know.''

"You do?''

"Sort of.''

"His father beat him with a chain sometimes. He'd come home all drunk and crazy and he'd take a chain to him.''

"Oh, God! He said a belt.''

"Oh, he would. Anything to make it less. To make like his father wasn't that bad. And he wasn't! He wasn't! Oh, honey, he wasn't. He was hurt, too. We all were.''

"Why . . . why didn't you leave? Why didn't you just grab Emily and Adam and go? Can I ask you that?''

"Oh, I thought of it all the time. But I was afraid. Because he threatened me if I talked about leaving. And the children, too. And I had nowhere to go. This

163

was my pa's house. And my grandpa's house. All the way back. It's *me*, this house. My home. Our home. And I'm not your modern woman. I was afraid to go out to get a job; I don't know anything.''

"Couldn't you have called the police?"

"I did. Once. It only made it worse, once the police was gone . . . And then, he was making illegal liquor and I didn't want the police to find out and put him in jail. Maybe I was wrong, but . . . anyway, he and his friend made liquor up here at night, and sold it. And he got drunk even more. And angry even more. It's what made Adam—oh, I don't know how to say it— so mixed up and strange. . . .''

"You mean like Vega-X?" I asked.

"All those stories he has."

"He believes them, doesn't he?"

"Honey, I wish I knew. And then, sometimes, he wakes at night, hollering and crying! And when I ask him what it is he won't say.''

"Did you ever think of, well, taking him to a psychologist?" I knew Mrs. Gladdings had said that Adam's mother didn't believe in them, but there was no harm trying. Maybe I could make a dent.

"Oh, that's all mumbo jumbo. Besides, I don't have any money for that.''

"There are free ones."

164

"I don't know about things like that. It's all mumbo jumbo, anyway."

"But he said he has nightmares. And I remember, he told me about a dream he had about that space capsule, and that he was inside it when he was little. That's the sort of stuff I think psychologists can help with."

"Oh, I know all about that dream! I told Adam where it came from, but he won't listen."

"What do you mean?"

"Something got stuck inside the still one time, the still for the liquor. And they slipped Adam in through a big hole, like a porthole, to unplug it. He was such a skinny little kid. But smart. So he got in and fixed it up."

"A still? Adam's capsule was a still for making moonshine whiskey?"

"Well I must have told Adam a hundred times! The government agents got onto it, and there was going to be a big raid, and somehow my husband got wind of it. So he and his friend went and buried the whole kaboodle. They dug all day and night and buried it. That was the end of the moonshining, thank heaven."

Oh, was I glad I'd stayed to talk. Maybe Mrs. Bates couldn't make Adam admit the truth, but I knew I could. That's why he didn't want to dig the capsule out: the space capsule would have turned into a still, before his eyes.

"Can I tell Adam that I know about this?" I asked.

"I don't see why not, honey. You know about everything else. He's a good, good boy, Lisa. He's been hurt real bad, that's all it is. . . ."

"I know."

"He'll be so glad to see you. He hasn't been himself at all."

"I haven't been myself at all, either," I said. "I guess none of us have. Don't worry, Mrs. Bates. Things are going to be okay."

17

I GOT ON my bike and headed toward the road, then doubled back, out of sight of the house, toward that clearing. I couldn't take my bike into the woods, so I hid it in a spot where I could find it later. I couldn't wait to see Adam; I ran over gullies and debris like a nut. I caught myself smiling, anticipating how I would smile the moment Adam saw me.

And there he was, exactly where Emily had said, sitting leaning against a tree, reading a book. He looked up and waved. "H-hi, Lisa!" He was supposed to be in tears, or something. But he wasn't. It was

167

almost as if he was expecting me.

"Hi, Adam," I said a bit warily.

"Hi. What's h-happening?"

What's *happening*? I couldn't believe it! He was as chipper as a church mouse. What was going on?

Then I heard a slight titter from the undergrowth nearby. Then two titters in chorus. So *that* was it! Emily and Cathy had beat me to the punch. Adam had been prepared.

"Thank you for coming, L-lisa." He was being serious now. "Thank you."

"You don't have to thank me. Stop always thanking me. Hi!"

Then from the bushes came the voice of one Emily Bates. "Kiss him!"

"Em-Emily! Go home! You too, Cathy."

"No! Kiss first! Come on! Please?"

I looked at Adam and shrugged. He shrugged back and blushed. Good old Adam, he's the best blusher I've ever seen. "What the heck!" I said. "Let's live a little." I went over and kissed him, a nice polite kiss on the lips.

"Yeaahhh!" came two voices from the bushes. Then Emily and Cathy leaped out and jumped on top of Adam. He lifted them both up by their waists and carried them, one under each arm, to the path in the

168

woods that led back to their house, while I followed. He was really strong. No wonder there had been broken noses and missing teeth. He carried them along the path a short way, while both girls roared with laughter. Then he dumped them down on the ground.

"Now, please go home! And don't tell Ma I'm here or I'll be in t-trouble."

"One more kiss," Emily called. "A mooshy mooshy kiss."

"Good-bye, Em-Emily!"

"Awww."

"Emily!"

"One mooshy!"

"Let's do it," I said. I really wanted to be alone with him, and it looked like we'd be stuck with Emily and Cathy all day. So we kissed again, and this was a real one. They *yeaahh*'d again and left.

"Hello, Adam," I said quietly.

"Hello, L-lisa."

"I'm crazy to tell you, but I really missed you, Adam. And I've been worried about you. Why didn't you come to school?"

"I didn't f-feel like it."

"Oh . . . Because of me?"

"Yes."

"Oh."

169

"I'm sorry, Lisa. I'm really sorry. I'll never take anything again."

"I'm calmer now. I'm older and wiser, okay? Your apology's accepted."

"It is?"

"Yes."

"Really!"

"Yes. Yes. Really."

"Thank you! Lisa? Are we f-friends again?"

"Of course."

"Like before?"

"Sure."

He swarmed over me, his arms around me, and held me and hugged me, rocking slightly, as if I were a long-lost child. I think he was crying a little, but I couldn't see.

"Lisa," he said finally, "I like you a lot."

"I like you a lot, too. I can't stop thinking about you. So I must like you a lot. And I do."

"I . . . I l-love you."

Oh, boy! Hey, Adam, I've only known you a few weeks! This was big-game territory we were in. But I felt it. And I couldn't *not* say it, so I said it. "I love you, too, Adam. You stupid jerk." I couldn't believe that two days ago I'd been ready to split for good. Maybe I'd known all along, that I wouldn't. . . .

170

We stood there hugging; it could have been for hours. Two against the world. All we needed were some violins. Or maybe a full orchestra. I can't help it; I laugh at myself, even at moments like this. Falling in love—ridiculous, right? Wrong! I was in love, and I loved it! I guess I'd been in love all along. Nuts to the world! I was in love! Let me tell you, I was feeling like a woman, not a kid, and I could feel, as we hugged, that Adam was feeling like a man, and I wasn't embarrassed one bit, and neither was he. We just hugged and hugged. And even touched a little, gingerly.

But all good things must come to an end, so I gently pushed free. I had this thought, and I burst out laughing.

"What's wrong?" Adam asked. "Are you l-laughing at me?"

"No. No. At something Kim said the other day. You see, I just twisted out of reach—*your* reach. We've got to talk. About a lot of things."

"Okay. Later."

"No, now. Adam, we've got to talk."

"Okay."

"Please. Let's sit down." We flopped on the ground, and Adam tried to put his arms around me again. "No, not like that! I really mean *talk*. Talk talk, not kiss talk."

171

"Okay. You start . . ."

"Well, first of all, I saw your mother, before, on the way up here. I thought you'd be at your house. Anyway, we spoke awhile, your mother and I. About how your father once had a still. And how you had to climb inside, one time, when you were little, and fix something. And later on, your father and his friend thought they'd get caught, so they buried the whole thing."

"I know. Ma keeps m-making up that story."

"*She's* making up a story!"

"She's afraid that I'm crazy, so she made up a story. She doesn't understand."

"Adam, look. Why don't we dig up the still or capsule or whatever it is, and see what's there."

"We can't. There's huge rocks on top of it."

"Is it really asking too much to give up that Vega-X story? You don't have to pretend anything with me. Please Adam, give it *up!*"

"I would . . . but I can't. It must be true if I can't. It is true. I know it is. It's like—I wouldn't ask you to say your name is J-Jennifer. Or Donna. Because it's Lisa. Right?"

"You believe it's true—let me follow this—you believe the story about Vega-X is true because you can't give it up? It sounds like you're on some sort of drug."

172

"No, you've said it backward. I can't give it up because it's true!"

"That's not what you said just now."

"It's what I m-meant! But listen! From now on, I swear, I won't talk about it. Okay? I won't say anything about Vega-X anymore. Okay? Lisa?"

"Well, it's a start."

"Okay. And you don't talk about twisting—what you said before."

"Twisting out of reach?"

"Right."

"Oh, yes I will! That's the other thing we have to talk about. Because the way we were going before . . . I don't want to have to start worrying about, you know, things like having a baby. Baby!"

"I wouldn't do that! I just like to h-hold you!"

"Oh. Well. In that case. Look out, baby!" I flung my arms around him again, very Hollywood, and we kissed for another ten hours or so—read: ten minutes—until we were all kissed out, if that's possible. Then we headed back down to get my bike where I'd left it.

I won't say much about the super sensation my photos made on Adam, Emily, and Mrs. Bates. You can guess. They loved them. Mrs. Bates tacked all the duplicate prints I gave her up on the walls, right then and there. They really went wild over them, I must modestly say. But there was more.

173

Mrs. Bates kept glancing at Adam and me holding hands. She smiled so much I thought her cheeks would burst. Then, at a certain moment, when I automatically gave Adam this little peck on the cheek, a super-quick kiss, her eyes flooded and she cried, standing there. It was one of those absolutely nutty scenes; we all just stood there and watched her cry. Then Emily cheered her mother on, the same way she'd cheered our kisses in the woods. *"Yeaahhh!"* Because Emily knew, we all knew, that she was crying from happiness.

18

I WAS ON A high. So many good things were happening at once. In the days that followed our big scene in the woods Adam and I were together every afternoon, at the library, at the mall, at Green Lake. And not a word about Vega-X or any other planetary system, near or far. And that *what's happening* sense of humor was there—slightly nutty, but I liked it. One day, Adam bought me a flower, a single rose. I think it used up every cent he had. After I had flipped over it he said, in all seriousness, that he had to take it back; he'd rented it for an hour, and I was only allowed three

175

sniffs. When I took a fourth sniff, he pinched my nose with his fingers.

"No! Don't! W-we'll both go to jail!" he'd shouted. "They can tell!"

On the Saturday of Memorial Day Weekend we were together all day with Kim and Russ, first at Green Lake, then for some el cheapo Chinese food at the mall, then a movie about the real story of Tarzan. We missed a lot of the plot because we were all busily necking in the last row. The only sad note is that Adam had still refused to take his T-shirt off at the lake; he swam with it on. But, oh, could he swim! Incredible!

Russ really seemed to like Adam; this time there'd been no wise remarks. Was it Adam's lifesaving last weekend that had done it, or had Kim told Russ more than I might have liked about Adam? I wasn't sure, but if it had civilized the Hulk, so be it. Russ was even acting nicer to Kim.

During all this, every free evening, I worked on preparing my final enlargements for the contest. I'd selected two dozen, then boiled them down to fourteen absolutely great shots. I redid one of them eleven times, burning in, changing development times, changing the paper, the solution, on and on, for the perfect "ten." And finally, I had it: Adam swinging Emily up in the air, with the house beyond, and a tangle of clouds

176

above—everything clean, clear, right. And that extra something. The thing, whatever it is, that makes my hair stand on end.

I *am* going to be a photojournalist. I *am*! I knew it as I worked. I knew it when I laughed and cried at some of the shots. I knew it when the eleventh trial hit the jackpot. I didn't have to win a contest. I felt it inside my belly and my brain. This was me—rip it away, and you'd rip away my right side.

The only fly in my ointment was Mom. She was down again. Since my reconnection with Adam, so stupidly announced in front of Mrs. Freeman, Mom had been morose. That's the correct word, morose— you have to pout to say it. Maybe that's how the word morose got started. Like smile. You have to smile to say *smile*.

Mom was depressed, and this time I felt it was *me* all the way. Not Dad, *me*. Every time I saw her I felt guilty for depressing her, and then I resented being made to feel guilty. Why should I feel guilty about going out with Adam? Why was she doing this? She'd actually been on a high of sorts when I'd been crying and seemingly splitting with him. But, now that I was *up*, she was *down*! Is there a psychiatrist in the house?

I tried to tell her all was well. Adam and I were not doing anything, Mom! It didn't matter. I was seeing

177

him; that was enough. Yet she didn't try to stop it; I guessed she was stuck for a first-rate, solid, airtight objection. Besides which, Dad had decided that he kind of liked Adam, just from those photos he'd seen. Irrational, but I wasn't about to argue.

Because of Mom, I decided I'd better not ask Adam to come over to our house for a while. I explained to him that Mom was giving me a very hard time for this and that reason, none of them connected to him, and he seemed to understand. He did say *I guess she d-doesn't like me* at one point, but I reassured him that, no, it was me. Not to worry; it was all in the family. It would pass like a summer storm.

But still, all in all, things were going beautifully. I handed in my fourteen enlargements, mounted on cream-colored boards, the day before the May 31 deadline. Mrs. Nicholson, my favorite librarian, seemed happy that I was "in." She knew me well from the piles of photography books that I'd borrowed and reborrowed, ad infinitum. Last year I'd taken a flash picture of her standing behind the big main desk, then mounted it and gave it to her for Christmas. I think I'll do that for a lot more people this year.

Anyway, I'd decided not to show the final enlargements to anyone, including Adam. All the entries were to be displayed in the library, and I wanted everyone to see the series up on the walls. That's when you really get the full impact. I know, because I'd put them up in my room for a trial run.

So things were going well. The Lake Hills graduation dance was looming over the horizon, only three weeks away. Kim had reminded me to tell Adam that he was going with me, or else! The truth is, I didn't want to go. I don't really know how to dance. Kim had tried to teach me once—more than once—but it was like trying to teach a duck how to waltz. The image isn't too far off; just picture me with feathers and you've got it.

But, when I told Adam about it, down at Green Lake, he said *yes*. He had never danced in his life, but that didn't stop Adam. I guess he thought I wanted to go.

"I can get a book from the l-library," he said. "I can learn how."

"From a book!"

"Sure."

"Okay. Great. But I warn you, I'll take pictures of you doing it, with that book in your hand. You know me. The camera nut. I'll take pictures of anything that won't bite back."

"That's because you're w-weird, Lisa, same as me. But maybe, you know, there are some things you can't take pictures of."

179

"Oh, really? What, for example?" I asked, a little belligerently. I guess I was bracing for another trip to Vega-X.

"This," he said, taking my hand and squeezing it. "This."

He meant, of course, the feeling, the togetherness, the *it*; that part of existence where words stop and pictures fail. The insight seemed beautiful to me. It's what makes Adam, Adam. But I still had to stand up for the art of the camera, because I think a great photo can show *those* things, too.

"Wait till you see my final prints," I said, not willing to concede. "They're putting them up in the library on Wednesday. You'll eat your words, Adam, baby."

"But there aren't any words," he said, and kissed me very gently on the lips. "S-see?" Then he kissed me again, even more gently.

I saw. At that moment, it was game, set, and match to Adam.

19

I FINALLY BLEW my cool on Wednesday morning, the
day the photos were to go up at the library. It was at
breakfast. The Lake Hills *Daily Sentinel* had a half-
page spread describing the photo exhibit and contest.
And more—they'd listed the names of everybody in
the contest in fine print. Including me, folks, in the
photo essay category. Only they spelled my name Lisa
Danies, leaving out the "l." My first tiny claim to
fame, and somebody had to mess up.

The photos were to be hung that morning, while I
was at school, and I had no idea how they'd treat my

babies. I didn't even know if they'd display all four-teen. That's a lot of wall space for one contestant.

"I see you made the papers," Dad said at breakfast. "Congratulations."

"Oh, that's nothing," I answered. "Everybody's listed."

"And some even have their names spelled right," said Mom. How crabby can you get!

"And happy Wednesday to you, too, Mother."

Dad intervened, as usual. "Hey, come on, you guys! Not again! Come on, cool it! Phyllis, give her a break. This is a big day for her."

"I merely commented on the typos in our daily paper," Mom said. "I didn't blame you for it, Lisa. I think you can spell your own name by now. Most of the time."

"Okay, Mom. Sorry. I didn't understand." She was still pretty clipped and snippy, but I wanted peace.

"We'll be going to see it, first chance we have," she said.

"Soon as I get home from work this evening," said Dad. "What time does the library close?"

"I think nine," I said.

"Good."

"Your friend is in those pictures, isn't he?" asked Mom.

182

"Some of them. Yes," I said. "Why?"

"Just curious. So that boy is in them. That's all."

"You *know* he is. And his name is *Adam*, not *that boy*!"

"I know what his name is," said Mom.

"Well, then why don't you say it. It won't kill you. His name is Adam!"

"Don't you shout at me!"

"I'm tired of this garbage! Why can't you say his name!"

"Lisa, watch how you talk to Mom!" Dad rose up from his chair.

"You're boycotting him!" I shouted to Mom. "You are! You won't even say his name! You don't like him, and you're treating him like an outcast! And I'm tired of it! You won't talk! You won't say what's wrong with him! All you do is—"

"I'll tell you what's wrong with him!" Mom shouted back. "He's a thief! There, is that better! He's a thief! Your *Adam* is a thief!"

Oh, boy. She'd known all along. Why hadn't she said anything? What was *with* her?

"Okay, Mom. Very good. Do you feel better now?"

"You want to talk! *Talk!* Go ahead! Everybody's going to be late. Dad's going to miss his bus. But talk!"

183

"Adam . . . made a mistake. He thought, somehow, that he could have one of the paperweights. It was just a misunderstanding. He . . . gave it back to me."

I was lying. I didn't care. Her holding back what she knew was sort of a lie, too. I looked at Dad. He didn't have the foggiest idea of what we were talking about. Mom hadn't told him. Didn't they talk? Mom was on some trip of her own. I felt my world getting shaky. It was more than just Adam. Maybe it was them. Maybe it was us, as a family.

"He gave it back to you, did he?" Mom continued. "And is that why you came home crying your head off? Is it?"

"Mom, why didn't you say something? Why? Not even to Dad?"

"I wanted *you* to say something. And you didn't. Why couldn't you tell me about it yourself? I can't trust you for anything anymore. Not after this!"

"I didn't say anything because—because I knew—" I was fighting the tears now. "I knew—you'd react, just as you're doing. He's not a thief! He just didn't understand! It was for his sister. And, anyway, he's had such a rotten life! He—he was beaten by his father with a chain! His back is all—it's all . . . Oh, *please*! Can't you understand *anything*! He's so decent! Oh, Mom! Dad! He's so—decent! There are so many rats

184

in this world! And he's so . . . Oh, Mom. . . .''

I was crying. Mom was trying to look stern, but she was at the edge of tears, too, maybe for different reasons. It did make some sense, what she'd said a moment before about *my* opening up to *her*. I thought I'd gotten away with the whole stupid thing—but I'd been wrong. I guess that's why I was crying. But she didn't have to play me out like a fish, the way she'd done!

"All right, Lisa," Mom said, less angrily now. "He's been abused, and that explains some of it. And no doubt his parents are very poor. But it still doesn't excuse his—''

"Don't say it, Mom! He's not a thief! . . . If only you'd give him a chance."

Dad stepped in. "I'm not sure of every detail here, but I've gotten the drift. I want to meet Adam. Soon. I want to see what he's like. I'm saying it again, Phyllis, we have to let Lisa use her own head and her own feelings. I've got to go, and so do you, Lisa. We'll talk more about it tonight.''

Mom sat toying with her coffee spoon. She was upset, but she didn't seem angry anymore.

"If he had asked, I would have found an inexpensive one to give him," she said.

"I know you would have, Mom."

"You're the only child I have, Lisa."

185

"I know."

"Do you really like him that much?"

"Yes."

She sighed. It was a sigh of resignation, I guess. "Go to school. You're late."

I was. The school bus was gone. Dad drove me to school on the way to his bus station. He didn't say much in the car, but as I got out he said, "Take it easy on Mom. She loves you, believe it or not."

"I know she does."

"And so do I. Believe it or not."

"Oh, Dad, I know you do."

"One other thing. Stick to your guns, kid. I think you're dynamite."

Oh, Dad!

20

WE ALL PLANNED to meet in front of the Lake Hills Library at three-thirty sharp. Note: I said in front of, because we planned to all go in together, the *artiste* and her coterie. And that included not only Adam and Kim, but Russ. I'm not sure whether Russ was interested in the art of photography so much as in seeing the kind of shack Adam lived in, but he was coming, too.

"Yeah, I'll be there, aright?" he mumbled.

"Aright, aright," I'd mumbled back, doing a little reverse tit-for-tat imitation to soothe my soul. Russ did not catch it at all.

I must have mentally rearranged the sequence of my prints two dozen times in the course of that school day, but it was too late. I'd handed in my requested sequence at the time I'd submitted the photos. The one with Adam swinging Emily was the last, my closing kicker, and that was the only one I wouldn't have switched around even if I'd still had the choice.

All day, my thoughts rose and fell on waves of anxiety. And it wasn't about Dad meeting Adam; I knew Dad would like him. I had not a worry in the world about that. It was the stupid photos. Would they put them all up? Would they be in some hidden corner? Would they look rank amateur against the work of adults?

Never, ever, had I seen clock hands move so slowly. Even my digital watch seemed to have lost its mind. It couldn't be only eleven-thirty! Good grief!

I had lunch with Adam; he was eating with me now instead of with the resource-room kids, and I could see that Mrs. Gladdings was glad. I wonder if someone could do a transfusion from Gladdings to Felts, a sort of smile transfer. Anyway, there we were, having lunch together in our far corner of the cafeteria, two lovebirds chewing their special hero sandwiches in perfect harmony.

With his mouth full of hero, Adam silently pushed

the latest library book he was reading toward me. It was *The Art of Photojournalism*. I'd read that one a half dozen times, but I'd never mentioned it to him. He was great!

And the clock waltzed on, minute by endless minute. When two-thirty finally arrived, I rushed to the school bus for no good reason, since it stood there for another five minutes before it took off.

Once home, I raced inside, dumped my backpack, and grabbed an apple. Mom wasn't there; she worked at the daycare center on Wednesdays. I wrote a note on the pad in the kitchen:

Dear Mom—Am at library with Kim, etc., for exhibit opening. We may celebrate with pizza, etc. Please don't hold supper for me. Your dutiful daughter, The Thing.

It may not sound like it but that was my way of saying: Mom, I'm sorry for driving you nuts. I was even careful to substitute that first *etc.* for Adam, so as not to rub her the wrong way with the note. Was I being thoughtful or neurotic? In households like mine you can't separate one from the other.

I got to the library at ten after three and rode my bike back and forth, till Kim arrived around twenty-five after. It was all I could do to not go inside.

Kim and I chained our bikes together in the parking

189

lot, and I took my small Minolta camera out of my pannier. I was planning to take some shots, just for fun, of all of us looking at my prints, and of the general exhibit. That's the way it goes; when you're a true camera bug, you end up taking pictures of yourself taking pictures of pictures.

"Nervous, Lee Lee?" asked Kim.

"Not a bit," I lied.

"Oh, yes you are. I can tell. You bite your lower lip when you're nervous."

"Oh, that's not nervousness. That's just an exercise to get in practice for Adam." Kim and I both laughed at that one. I'm getting to be terrible. Pretty soon I'll be writing messages on the sides of the carrels in the library. *Lisa loves Adam.* Some of those messages are unbelievably gross, I might add. Mrs. Nicholson and the other librarians must not examine those carrels very often.

Russ arrived, and Adam came pedaling up on his old coaster bike a minute later.

"H-hi!" He swung off his bike smoothly while it was still moving. Russ liked that, I could tell.

The moment had arrived. It was time for the grand entrance, with Adam's arm around my shoulder and Kim and Russ right behind in case I fainted or started floating up toward the ceiling.

It was great! The library looked like a New York

art gallery, with people going slowly from photo to photo. There were a bunch of kids I recognized from school, as well as some adults. I hadn't expected it; I'd thought we'd be the only ones at this hour. I guess the kids were there to do research projects; it was final-report time at Lake Hills. We walked farther in, and there, *there*, on the far wall, very visible, were my fourteen, count them, fourteen photos like a long passenger train. *Yahoo!* And there were some women studying them.

This I had to see. And hear. What were they saying? I motioned to Adam and the others to walk over quietly, and not speak. I got right behind the women and tuned in.

"Marvelous work," one of them said. Oh, joy!

"So moving. . . . Oh, look at her sitting in that big old armchair outdoors. What a wonderful, warm feeling."

It was Adam's mother in her armchair. Joy! Joy!

"Yes, and that boy swinging that little girl around. It's a poem."

Yes, it is! It is! Adam, did you hear that? I looked at him. He was blushing, but when he saw me he shyly smiled.

The women moved on. Stay! Say some more good things!

A bunch of boys came over and pushed their way

in front. I knew them vaguely from school. Russ nudged me.

"Better go," he said. "Come on. . . ."

It was too late. I will give you their dialogue, word for word, as I remember it. And I will say, for whatever it's worth, that they didn't seem to realize that Adam was right behind them.

"Look at that dump, man. What's it supposed to be?"

"It's an abandoned shack."

"No, look! See that guy in that picture? He's that retard from school. What a shithouse he lives in."

That imbecile! I grabbed Adam's hand and squeezed hard. "Let's go. We'll come back later," I whispered.

"I'm okay! I'm okay! That isn't my house," Adam said, very quickly, to me. "They p-put me there. To test me! To test me!"

Oh no! He was doing that planet bit again! That dumb, stupid planet bit!

"Man, how can anybody live in a dump like that? Hey, look at the lady in that beat-up chair. She must be the retard's mother."

"She isn't my mother." Adam said, under his breath. "They p-put me there. I'm okay. I'm okay."

Russ was looking at me, and so was Kim. "We've got to go," I said, and squeezed Adam's hand harder, trying to drag him away. But he resisted. Did he *want* to hear this garbage?

"His mother's gotta be the biggest slob I ever seen, sitting like that. She's falling out of her dress. Man, what a slut!"

And it happened, faster than I can describe. Adam pulled the guy's arm and spun him around. In that same moment, Adam's fist slammed against his jaw. The guy's head cracked against the wall, then he slid down to the floor, twisting one of my pictures sideways.

I couldn't stop Adam. Neither could Russ. Adam had grabbed a chair and was raising it over the guy's head, threateningly.

"No!" I called out.

Adam looked at me and his eyes were like gray bullets. He turned back toward the guy and his buddies—who looked pretty scared—then, with a sudden lunge, smashed the chair against the wall. It exploded into three pieces. The upper part shot across the room and ricocheted off a bookshelf.

Nobody moved except Adam. He turned one way then another, like a trapped animal, then pushed me out of the way and half ran, half stumbled out of the library. As he ran he gave out a sort of choked cry, not very loud, almost as if he were being smothered. "Uuhhh . . ."

I must have done a dozen things in that next thirty seconds. My first impulse was to run after Adam—

but if I didn't cool everything down at the library, he'd be wrecked! *We'd* be wrecked! My feelings were numbed out; I was working on nerve alone. A crowd was gathering around us.

The guy on the floor was shaking his head again and again; he must have been knocked unconscious for a few seconds. Good! He deserved it! But, my God, they might call the police. What could I *do*?

"Hey man, you okay?" asked Russ, helping him up.

"Yeah. Yeah," said the guy, holding his jaw.

"Hey, he didn't mean nothing. That was him, the guy in the picture." Russ was talking to all three boys at once.

"That was *him*? Oh, shit . . ."

"Yeah. Hey, forget about it, right? That was his mother. You know how it is. Forget about it."

"Oh, man . . . I didn't know he was right behind us. Oh man . . ."

"Yeah . . . right . . ."

Thank God for Russ! The Hulk knew these guys! And he knew how to talk to them. Oh, what a break! I didn't think any of the adults around had seen Adam punch the guy out. But there was still the wrecked chair to take care of.

Everyone in the library was around us by now, including the librarians.

194

"What happened here?" asked Mrs. Nicholson.

"Please. Please," I said, a bit hysterically. "Mrs. Nicholson, please. Let me talk to you a minute alone. Please let me talk."

"What happened to that chair?" she asked, as we moved away from the crowd.

"Please. My friends will clean it up. And I'm going to pay for it. I'll get the money today!"

"I don't understand. Why would you want to pay for it? Did you break it?"

"Yes! In a way . . ." I walked her farther away from the crowd. "What happened was, my friend was here. He's in those pictures."

"Do you mean Adam Bates?"

"Do you know him?"

"I ought to. He borrows half the books in the library."

"See, and those guys, they insulted him. And his mother. From those pictures. It was really bad."

"I can imagine."

"So he, you know, blew his cool. He broke the chair, but it was my pictures that did it. It was actually my fault. I'll pay for it. You aren't going to call the police, are you? It won't happen again."

"We're not going to call the police for a broken chair."

I was faint with relief. *Lucky* was the word that

repeated in my head. Lucky. What was everybody saying? I walked back to the crowd with Mrs. Nicholson and listened to her with one ear, while I tried to get the drift of what was being said, with the other. Mrs. Nicholson was actually trying to calm me down. From the crowd, I heard a buzz of *what happened*s and *why*s, but no one was saying police. Okay. Okay. Things were cool. It was under control.

I spoke to everyone, rapid fire. "Kim, I'm going over to Adam's. Mrs. Nicholson—how much—how much does a chair cost? Russ, thanks. Thanks. Kim, lend me the money, you know, for the chair, as much as you can, and I'll pay you back—"

Mrs. Nicholson had the pieces of the chair together by now. She pointed at the wall. "He put a dent in that wall,

"I'll—I'll fix it . . . or I can get someone . . . or—"

"Take it easy," she said. "Take it easy. If you want, you can come over and help us shelve books for a few Saturdays. And so can Adam. We're always short of help. I'll take care of that broken chair."

"Thank you, Mrs. Nicholson. Thanks an awful lot."

So there it was. I was back on square one yet again. Yet again! With Adam rocking everyone's boat—not that I didn't feel like smacking that rat-head myself. But in a public library! Good grief! And back, again,

196

with Vega-X—again! Every crisis, he drags out Vega-X. Vega-X and a fist to the jaw. Wonderful!

He was unstable. That's the word my mother used about my cousin in Florida. Unstable. I loved my cousin. I loved Adam. I did. I still did. But I could not, and I would not, keep cleaning up the mess after him. No way!

Don't ask me what I planned to do. I didn't know. I didn't even know if he'd gone back to his house. But I had to do something. So I just got on my bike and rode toward the hills, blindly, because it was better than going home and falling apart in front of Mom.

21

WHEN I GOT to Adam's house, nobody seemed to be home. There was no doorbell, so I banged on the front door for awhile. Nothing. I walked around and around the house, not sure of what to do next, hoping I'd spot Emily in the field. Nothing. Nobody.

I sat on that armchair in the backyard, with my feet sprawled out, waiting for someone to come, trying to think where to go next. The chair wasn't even comfortable, and it smelled from mildew.

I sat there for about five minutes, feeling like a trespasser. Then I went around to the front again, and

198

looked in through the kitchen window. The sink had some dirty dishes in it, and someone had left a bottle of milk on the table. Nothing else. I peeked through the window of Emily's room. Empty. Then I looked through a window of the main big room and, of course, there was Adam, curled up against the wall, his head down. Beautiful! Why hadn't he opened the door!

I rapped on the window and Adam looked up. Then he let his head go down again.

"Open up!" I shouted.

He didn't move.

"Open up, or I swear, I'll break this window open! Adam, you stupid bonehead, open up!"

He got up slowly and shambled toward the front door. The idiot!

"W-what do you want?" he said behind the closed door.

"Let me in! *Adam*!"

He unlatched the door, then started walking back toward the wall as I entered.

"Adam, I can't believe it! That idiot at the library was a total louse, but that didn't give you the right to punch him out and break up the place!"

"I don't care."

"You don't *care*! I had to—to beg the librarian to give you a break! Russ had to calm down the guy you punched! Everybody has to clean up the shit you leave behind! And you don't care!''

"Leave me alone!'' he shouted. "I d-didn't ask you to do anything! I didn't!''

"Adam, they could have called the police for that! Is this the way you're going to live your life? You stupid bonehead!''

"My life? What l-life is that?''

"What do you mean? You have your life ahead of you!''

"*This* is my life!'' he screamed at me. "Look around! L-look! You took those pictures! You ought to know! Everybody in the library knows! This dump is my life! This dump! You—you come here to tell *me*? You got your fancy rugs, and your p-p-paperweights, and your videos, and your soap that smells like a Christmas tree! And you're telling me about my life! This lousy broken-down trash can is my life!''

"Adam, your life is what's inside the skin of your body. Nothing else.''

"Bull! Bull! But I don't care. I don't care. See! You d-don't want me to say it, but I've got to say it. I was sent there, I *was*, and this is my test. I almost blew it! I almost blew it! This is the big test. I know it. I've got to take it easy. This is it. She isn't my m-mother. And Emily isn't my—''

200

"She *is* your mother! And she *is* your sister! And this *is* your house! And the only thing you ever have to be ashamed of—the only thing—is *being* ashamed of this."

"I don't care if you don't believe me. I d-don't care. . . ."

"You're right! I don't believe you!"

"I don't care!"

I had a sudden idea! I pictured it almost like a photo. That's how I think sometimes.

"Get ready, Adam! Because I'm digging up that capsule! Right now! You can come and watch!"

I remembered a rusty old shovel out in the yard with the other junk. Okay, Adam, I thought. Here we go! I got up and walked toward the door.

"You c-can't dig it out. It's too deep!"

"If two grown men can bury it in twenty-four hours, one teenaged female can dig it up in a week, and I'm going to dig it out if it takes me a month!"

I was on my way. I grabbed the shovel and, dragging it along the ground behind me, half walked, half ran through the field in back of the house, past the outhouse toward the woods. Adam followed me.

"It's too deep!"

"Good! I need the exercise!"

"There's big rocks! You need a backhoe."

201

"I'll rent one!"

"Lisa!"

I plunged on, with Adam galloping along beside me shouting *It's too deep. It's no use.* When we reached the clearing, I climbed onto the pile of branches and started throwing them aside. To my surprise Adam joined me, tossing the bigger branches. He was actually helping me. Helping me to prove he was wrong. Why? It was the same crazy, unbelievable, lovable Adam. He was helping me, the jerk! Or did he just possibly *want* me to prove he was wrong?

With the copper hemisphere exposed, I started digging around the edge. I could hardly get the shovel into the ground, the soil was so hard packed. And there *were* rocks; every time the shovel struck the ground, there were little sparks as metal hit stone.

"I'm not stopping till it's done!" I shouted.

Adam sat on a nearby log and stared at me, and I must say, he looked totally miserable. Every time my shovel made its sharp crack against the ground he blinked, as if I was shooting off a pistol.

After a few minutes I'd actually managed to hollow out a small crater near one edge of the hemisphere. "I'll say it again, Adam!" I shouted. "I'm not going to go on with this crap anymore!"

Adam had picked up a handful of small pinecones

from the ground and started tossing them at me, one at a time. One of them hit me on the back of the hand, and it stung.

"Cut it out! Why don't you just punch me in the face, like that guy in the library?"

He kept lobbing the pinecones, like tiny hand grenades. After a while I began to realize that he was aiming at the copper sphere, not me.

I kept on digging, but the handle of the shovel was rubbing the skin raw between my thumb and forefinger. "This shovel is no damn good!" I shouted. "I need a pick! And I'm going to get one! I swear I'll bring one up here! I'm not going to let anything stop me!"

I continued to dig, though every swing of the shovel hurt my hand now. Adam dropped the pinecones and came over. He took the shovel from my hands, swung it around at arm's length, and hurled it into the woods.

"I'm going to go after it! You're not going to stop me, you stupid—" I punched him on his chest, as he tried to grab my arm. "Let go of me! I'm going to get that shovel and dig the thing out!"

He succeeded in getting my arm. "L-lisa, stop a minute! Please!"

"Are you going to punch me out now? Go ahead! That'll do it, once and for all! Go ahead!"

"It's—it's a . . . L-lisa, listen!"

203

"What do you want now!"

"It's a s-still. . . . It's a still."

"Oh, brother . . . oh, brother . . . Say it again, what you just said."

"That capsule's a still. Okay? Okay? Are you s-satisfied? *Okay?*"

"Okay. Adam? *Really*, Adam?"

"Yes."

"Oh, Adam—I—you're not going to change it on me, are you? Are you?"

"No." He was staring at the ground as if he were ashamed to look me in the eye.

"Is—is your mother your mother? And everything?"

"Yes . . . you know she is."

"Can't you look at me?"

He didn't move. I went over and raised his head. His eyes were narrow slits.

"I d-don't want to see you anymore. . . ."

"What! Why? Now, maybe, we can really begin!"

"You've seen what I really am. I'm garbage. I don't want to s-see you anymore."

"You think I care that you actually live here and didn't come from never-never land?"

"Yes."

"Are you out of your skull! Birdbrain! I love you

for this and this and this!'' I pressed my hand against his forehead and mouth and chest.

"No . . . no. You're rich. . . . Your mother doesn't l-like me. I can tell, And I'm—I'm just garbage.''

"Is this going to be your new song and dance? Adam?''

"It's true and you know it. You're the one with the camera. Take a picture of *that*! Okay? I'm garbage.''

"You can't just be your own self, can you! If you're not from Vega-X, then you're no damn good. You've got a new song and dance. Birdbrain!''

Then I suddenly had another idea. Another photo-flash. It was my day for ideas. This one was a little scary, but . . . I grabbed Adam's hand. "Come on, let's go,'' I said. "I'm going to make my point, or drop dead trying.''

"Where are you going?''

"You'll find out! I think I know the way. Come on, birdbrain!''

"Don't call me that!''

"I'll call you that till you stop acting like one. Let's go!''

I headed through the woods, in the direction we'd come that first day when I'd gotten off Adam's bus with him. I circled past his house and down that narrow path, with Adam right next to me. Every time he asked

205

what was going on, I said that he was a birdbrain.

When we got to Adam's pond, the one he'd done his underwater aquashow in, I stopped, then walked over to the edge. I felt the water with my hand.

"Getting warmer. Okay. Let's swim, Adam!"

"You want to swim?"

"Right on, baby! Strip, Adam! Cause that's what I'm doing!" And without missing a beat, I started getting out of my clothes. Yes, I was plenty uptight, but I was going to do it, and that was that. "Come on, Adam. You said you would. This is your moment!"

And we stripped. And plunged in. The water was still unbelievably cold to me, but I was so spaced out with what I was doing, that it didn't register that much. We splashed around, and Adam dived under. I tried to, also, for maybe ten seconds.

"Hey, Adam!" I called as we surfaced. "You said I'm rich, before. Where is it? All this wealth?"

"At your house . . ."

"I'm here! Right here! This is me! No more, no less! Right? And this is you, no more, no less! This is *us*, birdbrain! And if somebody catches us, we'll both be thrown in the clink. If you're garbage, then I'm garbage, too. Okay? Got it? *This* is all of you, birdbrain. Not your house. Not your outhouse. Not your clothes. Not your mother, though I like her. Not even Emily, though I like her, too. *You* are what is in this lake. And *I'm* what's in this lake. The rest is bull. Do you understand? Birdbrain? Birdbrain?''

"You don't have to skinny-dip to t-tell me . . .''

"Maybe I do! Because you aren't listening! I'm not ashamed to strip in front of you. Why should you be ashamed, in front of me? I mean ashamed of your house. Or your yard. Or your family. Or your back. Or any of that bull. You see, birdbrain?''

"Maybe . . .''

"Oh, come on, Adam!''

"Okay . . . I see . . . that it doesn't matter . . . to you. Okay?''

"You're hedging. But, okay. Are you sure you see?''

"Yeah.''

"Okay! *Birdbrain* is hereby deleted. Key in *Adam*! Now let's get the hell out, *Adam*, because I am freezing!''

We got out, and I was very tempted to give him a huge hug, totally starko, but I resisted, with the famous words *one thing leads to another* spinning in my naked cranium. So I tossed Adam's jeans to him, and we got dressed.

"I wish we had towels," I said. "But I didn't exactly plan this."

207

"Yeah . . . Lisa, I guess you really l-like me, don't you?"

"Isn't it obvious? Don't make me say *birdbrain* again."

"Hey, Lisa. I don't think we should tell anybody what we just did . . . even though everybody d-does that on Vega-X."

Yes, he was smiling. But I still jumped a little.

"Adam, please. Don't even kid about Vega-X."

"Okay . . . Hey, Lisa . . . I like the way you looked—you know—before, in the lake. You looked b-beautiful. I mean it."

"Thanks. So did you. . . . Too bad I didn't have my camera at the ready."

And we kissed a little and hugged a little, and walked back to Adam's house arm in arm. And for the first time, it was simply Adam and Lisa, and Lisa and Adam, and no pebbles in my shoe, no little thorn in the side of my brain. I don't really know exactly how it had happened, exactly what magic button had done it, not just for Adam, but for me, too. But life being what it is, I take what I can get, and ask questions later.

22

THEY WERE GETTING ready to tear down Adam's house.
Adam and I were in the field behind, watching as the
big yellow machine moved into position. The roar of
the bulldozer was everywhere; the echoes seemed to
come out of the ground, and out of the hills, and out
of the sky.

Mrs. Bates and Emily hadn't come; they'd stayed
down in the mobile-home park. Mrs. Bates didn't want
to come. I don't blame her. Emily's made some new
friends; I think the move's been good for her. But Mrs.
Bates just hates the whole thing. And Adam doesn't
say a word.

209

It was hot, even for August. I was glad I'd had the sense to bring a jug of orange-juice ice cubes. As you suck them, lo and behold, you've got ice-cold orange juice. And I'd brought two cameras. I'd taken half a dozen shots already, including two of Adam in front of the bulldozer.

This fall they're going to put up a storage facility there. It's been zoned for industry; some company wants a remote site to store undoubtedly dangerous chemicals.

The bulldozer started lifting the pile of tires, Emily's jungle gym of tires, into a huge green dump truck. They were starting nice and easy with the loose stuff first. Very humane.

So there we were, sitting cross-legged, like little kids watching a parade or a magician. I'd even brought some sandwiches. What was the use of starving?

In the two months since that wild day at the library and the pond, Adam hasn't said a word about Vega-X and neither have I. I think he wants to forget about Vega-X.

I'd hoped Adam would join the Lake Hills community swim team; I'd gently suggested it several times, and he'd finally agreed to go down for the summer tryouts. In the first trial heat, he'd won by a mile. His strokes looked crazy—he said he'd learned them from a book—but he tore through the water like a whale with a rocket tied to its rear. But, for the second trial, they asked him to take off his T-shirt. And, of course, he refused. The coach asked him again, very loud and clear. *Take off the lousy T-shirt or get off the swimming dock!* Adam got off the dock, and that was that.

Since then, I've tried to get him to swim at Green Lake without that T-shirt, but he won't. Still, last Sunday, Adam and I went down to the Jersey shore with my parents—yes, my parents, believe it or not!—and I walked with him to a far end of the beach where we couldn't possibly know anybody, and he did take off that stupid shirt for a few minutes.

I have great hopes for the fall and the high school swim team. He says maybe he will. I don't know.

As you can guess, Adam comes to my house now. And Mom is polite. Dad is friendly; Mom is polite. I'll buy polite; it's a lot better than the cold shoulder, not to mention the cold hip, I thought he'd get. She was polite in the car on the way to the shore, and at the shore, and on the way home. The trouble is, she's being polite to me, too. I wish she'd blow her stack once, so I could blow mine in return. Maybe then we could be sort of friends again, instead of walking on egg shells. But I can see she's trying. Dad

211

got her to go for counseling and, in fact, they've been going together, lately. I think she's been less depressed. And she's cut down on the martinis, too. That's something.

I stood up and took more shots of the bulldozer as it raised its maw high up in the air with an old oil drum in it. *KABAAM!* The oil drum crashed down into the dump truck. Adam just sat there with his arms around his knees, looking a little dazed.

His mother had gotten a lawyer, a free one for people on welfare, but the lawyer couldn't stop the eviction. And my photo series hadn't made a dent in the real world. Even though the *Daily Sentinel* did a story on the contest and showed two of my photos, nobody in power seemed to care. Oh, I almost forgot—out of pure modesty, of course. I, L. Daniels, Inc., won second prize in the photo-essay division. Naturally, I was slighty biased and thought I should have come in first, but second wasn't bad for my first try. Mom and Dad came to the award ceremony and I think they were really proud of me. The only thing is, I wish Grandpa could have been there, too.

I blew the entire fifty-dollar prize on a celebratory Japanese meal with Adam and Emily and Adam's mother. It took a lot of coaxing but his mother finally agreed to go. We had a ball. It was one of those Japanese restaurants where they do all those tricks with the knives while preparing the food, right in front of your eyes, on this huge table-length griddle.

Guess who picked us up and drove us there? And also drove us back? Dad. The one and only. He even slipped me an extra twenty in case I got caught short.

So Adam and I have become, somehow, entangled. We've become part of each other's lives. For now. For this summer. For this moment in the galaxy. *This* galaxy, not the never-never land one. And we've done a lot of things together. Not *that*, friends. I mean things like the graduation dance, which was a lot of fun by the way. And we've gone biking, and picnicking, and even into New York once.

Adam had loved my New York tour. We'd started down in Chinatown where we had dim sum—those little trays of food they bring around—then we went to Tower Records, the three-story humongous record place, then to all the nutty clothing stores along Lower Broadway, then to that barbershop in the East Village where they give the punk haircuts and you can watch at the big window. That's a show in itself. Then we went across to Fifth Avenue by way of Washington Square Park—where we watched the jugglers, and street comedians, and that guy who swallows fire—then went all the way up Fifth, past the library and Rocke-feller Center, to the Museum of Modern Art, where we ended up, naturally, in the photo exhibit section. I guess I wanted Adam to see that what I was doing was an art, like painting or sculpture.

For Adam, our whole New York trip was like Columbus discovering America. Though it's only an hour by bus, he had been to Manhattan only once in his entire life, a class trip to the Museum of Natural History. I could see him soak up New York through his pores, the same way he soaks up those books in the library. We plan to go in once more before school starts in September, if Mom and Dad will let me. That first time I had to phone Mom every three hours, long distance, to tell her I was still alive. Next time should be easier.

And Adam's been laughing more, I think, and being silly sometimes, which is great. Though every so often he gets that look, that sad, lost look I'd noticed when I first met him. If I ask him what's wrong, he just shrugs and says *I'm okay. I'm okay.* He doesn't talk about himself, that's for sure. I wish he would.

The bulldozer had cleaned out most of the junk in the backyard. The huge green truck was full and was driving away, bouncing up and down like a sumo wrestler over all the ruts and ditches. An empty truck roared up to take its place.

Adam sat there, staring at the bulldozer as it roared toward the shack. I wished I could read his mind; his mouth was open, as if he wanted to cry or shout, but couldn't. I stood up and took a couple of quick shots of him squatting on the ground.

As the bulldozer rammed against the side of the house, everything started folding sideways. The back door jumped off its hinges and flew out into the yard, the windows crackled like cellophane and collapsed, the roof started sliding down. I felt sick to my stomach; I had to bite my lip to concentrate. But I took shot after shot, moving around to the front side of the bull-dozer. When I looked back at Adam, his hands were clenched together in his lap. I turned my viewfinder toward him again, and took some shots, feeling like a cold killer with a camera lens. I should have been there, next to him, maybe comforting him. Instead, I was doing my thing, even though it hurt.

Well, that's what it takes, I thought. That's what it takes to be a photojournalist. Or an artist. And it *was* an art. Because these shots, I knew, with my earlier ones, were going to make a really powerful before-and-after series about the way the world is. About how things live and die. Like those spiders of mine—only

215

now it was a house, and a person, and a family, and a way of life.

The bulldozer climbed up onto the wrecked and fallen walls and slammed against the natural stone chimney, still standing upright in the middle of the wreckage. But the fireplace and chimney wouldn't come down. The bulldozer growled to a stop. It was as if the American Revolution had one victory more left in its bag, *this* victory against a modern monster, this defiance, this *Don't tread on me*! My fingers flew as I took shot after shot.

The bulldozer backed away, then plunged toward the chimney again, and again it resisted, though now the upper column of stones had moved sideways on its base. Once more the bulldozer charged, and the roar of the revved-up engine vibrated inside my chest cavity. This time the chimney trembled and curved into a graceful arc, and the stones came apart, hanging in the air for a second, like gray birds. Then the stones banged down in an angry avalanche, battering the wreckage underneath. A big puff of dusty soot rose up, like an Indian smoke signal calling distress, and it was finished.

I went back and sat down next to Adam, while the bulldozer growled and raised up chunks of debris, dropping everything into the waiting dump truck.

I put my hand over Adam's clenched hand.

"Are you okay?" I asked. "Maybe we ought to go."

"N-no . . . I want to watch it," he said. "That—that was the wall of my bedroom." He pointed toward the bulldozer as it banged its maw down to break up a piece of flat debris. "That's the other wall . . . over there."

"How can you be—I don't know—so calm?" I asked.

"Now maybe I can stop having n-nightmares," he said. "Now it's dead. . . ."

"Are they nightmares of your house?"

"About him. Him . . . See? It's like a f-funeral. For him . . ."

"Is he dead, your father? You never say."

"I don't know. But every night he beats me in my sleep . . . see? And then, every night . . . I kill him. I kill him in my sleep . . . I c-can't help it. . . ."

"Oh, Adam!" He needs help, I thought. He needs help.

"Don't worry. I'm okay . . . I'm okay . . ."

I put my arm around him and I held him, and I tried to rock him a little because there were tears all over his face now; I tried to rock him as if to show him that if he'd been *my* child, this is what *I* would have done.

217

And he'd *been* right, and he *was* right: there's things you can't shoot with a camera, or paint, or say; all you can do is sit and hold somebody, like I did in that field, and rock somebody, and hope he'll be all right; all you can do is maybe try a quick prayer, like I did that afternoon inside my head, over the roar of the bull-dozer.